## "I'd spend a we... and you'd gran...

D0510778

"If my terms were met."

He made it sound so easy. Bryn stared at the water drops darkening the white cloth, her mind strangely blank. No words, no sound, no light filtering through her brain. "And what are those terms…?"

"I want a long weekend with you. Four days. Three nights. City of my choosing."

She touched one of the damp drops on the tablecloth with her finger. "You want me to be your wife?"

"I want you to be my lover."

He smiled without a hint of warmth in his eyes. "I want to possess you, enjoy you at my leisure, and make you mine—completely mine again."

Hunger and awareness stirred inside her. He knew he could seduce her at the drop of a hat.

**Jane Porter** grew up on a diet of Mills& Boon® romances (reading late at night under the covers so her mother wouldn't see!). She wrote her first book at age eight and spent many of her high school and college years living abroad, immersing herself in other cultures and continuing to read voraciously. Now, Jane's settled down in rugged Seattle, Washington, with her gorgeous husband and two young sons. Jane loves to hear from her readers. You can write to her at PO Box 524, Bellevue, WA 98009, USA.

**Recent titles by the same author:**

THE ITALIAN GROOM
CHRISTOS'S PROMISE

# THE SHEIKH'S WIFE

BY
JANE PORTER

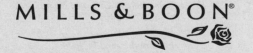

**DID YOU PURCHASE THIS BOOK WITHOUT A COVER?**

If you did, you should be aware it is **stolen property** as it was reported *unsold and destroyed* by a retailer. Neither the author nor the publisher has received any payment for this book.

*All the characters in this book have no existence outside the imagination of the author, and have no relation whatsoever to anyone bearing the same name or names. They are not even distantly inspired by any individual known or unknown to the author, and all the incidents are pure invention.*

*All Rights Reserved including the right of reproduction in whole or in part in any form. This edition is published by arrangement with Harlequin Enterprises II B.V. The text of this publication or any part thereof may not be reproduced or transmitted in any form or by any means, electronic or mechanical, including photocopying, recording, storage in an information retrieval system, or otherwise, without the written permission of the publisher.*

*This book is sold subject to the condition that it shall not, by way of trade or otherwise, be lent, resold, hired out or otherwise circulated without the prior consent of the publisher in any form of binding or cover other than that in which it is published and without a similar condition including this condition being imposed on the subsequent purchaser.*

*MILLS & BOON and MILLS & BOON with the Rose Device are registered trademarks of the publisher.*

*First published in Great Britain 2001
Harlequin Mills & Boon Limited,
Eton House, 18-24 Paradise Road, Richmond, Surrey TW9 1SR*

© Jane Porter 2001

ISBN 0 263 82534 5

*Set in Times Roman 10½ on 12½ pt.
01-0901-40562*

*Printed and bound in Spain
by Litografia Rosés, S.A., Barcelona*

# CHAPTER ONE

BRYN caught a glimpse of herself in the hall mirror as she headed toward the front door, the doorbell still ringing as she padded along the carpetless hall. Sheen of white dress, brilliant blue eyes, flushed cheeks. A radiant bride. And she did feel beautiful, more beautiful than she had in years. In just seven short days she'd be a bride again. She'd be Stanley's wife.

Smiling, Bryn hummed the wedding march as she swung the front door open, late-afternoon sunlight washing over her in streaky gold waves, briefly blinding her.

Blinking, she made out broad shoulders. The high curve of cheekbone. A beautifully shaped mouth. And only one man had that mouth. Her heart staggered to a stop. ''Wh…what…are you doing here?''

''Hello, darling. It's nice to see you, too.''

Time stopped, changed, and for a split second she was somewhere else, spellbound. It was just like the day she met him, the day she reversed her small Volkswagen, and slammed into his silver Mercedes Benz. Her car was totaled. His was merely dinged.

Bryn felt the impact again, the air knocked out of her lungs, her lips parting in shock. *''Kahlil.''*

''You remembered, good.'' He looked amused, but then, his gold eyes always smiled when he was angry.

Lifting a sheet of paper, he dangled it in front of her face. "Now perhaps you'll remember this," he drawled softly, giving the paper a gentle shake.

Bryn stared at the paper blankly, unable to read the words. Only his voice penetrated the muddle inside her head, his voice still husky, his English formal, the same English he'd learned as a child in an English boarding school. "What is it?"

"You don't recognize it?"

Her fingers felt nerveless as she clutched the door. "No."

Kahlil chuckled, the sound warm, indulgent, an indulgence he'd shown toward her early in their marriage when she'd been his prized American bride. "It's our marriage license. The little piece of paper that legally binds us together."

She couldn't speak, her throat swelling closed. He must be out of his mind, she thought, forcing herself to look into his face, meet his eyes.

He didn't look crazy. If anything he looked calm, perfectly controlled, as though he knew exactly what he was doing, as though he'd planned this surprise visit on purpose.

A week before her wedding…

Her thoughts spun, her brain fogged by shock and fear. What if Kahlil discovered Ben? *What if he found out about their son?*

No. She'd never go back to him. Never return to Zwar. Bryn drew herself tall, conviction making her back straight, her determination reinforcing her courage. "I don't understand what that has to do with us."

"Everything, darling." He was gazing down at her with considerable interest, thick black lashes fanning his carved cheekbones and the bronzed luster of his skin. "I've come to see why you're getting married again when you're still married to me."

Still married to him? Ridiculous. If he thought he could hoodwink her with a silly statement like that, then he had another thing coming. She wasn't eighteen anymore. She wasn't a child bride, either. "We're not married," she said crisply, disdain sharpening her voice. "We were divorced three years ago." How could he still refuse to accept their divorce? It'd been three years, more than three years. Three and a half years, actually. "I'm not in the mood for games. Perhaps in Zwar, divorces aren't permitted, but here they're perfectly legal."

"Yes, darling, I understand that much. And perhaps you've forgotten I have a law degree from Harvard, an *American* university, and despite my Arab nationality, I grasp the legality of an American divorce, but *we* were never divorced."

There was a quiet menace in his voice, a menace she heard all too clearly. Her head jerked up, her gaze clashing with his. "If this is your idea of a joke—"

"Have I ever been a comedian?"

No, she answered silently, bitterly. He was one man in desperate need of a sense of humor.

"I'm trying to prevent you further embarrassment,"

he added with the same infuriating calm. "I considered waiting until you'd arrived at the church, the guests filling the pews. I could just picture your eager groom at the altar, standing there in his black-and-white tux—he is wearing a tuxedo, isn't he?"

She couldn't bear to be the brunt of Kahlil's scorn. She'd witness him level others in the past, but never her. Kahlil had never been anything but protective, generous, *loving*.

Her heart squeezed on the last one, pained by the unwanted memory. Their marriage had been brief. Too brief but she couldn't go back, couldn't undo the past. "I think it's time you left."

He put his hand in the door to keep her from shutting it in his face. "I've tried to be polite, but perhaps it's better if I'm blunt. There will be no wedding next Saturday. And as long as I live, there will be no wedding to any man, ever."

She ground her jaw together, struggling to contain her temper. Maybe in his country men could veil their women, tell them how to dress, what to think, where to go, but not in the United States, and not in her home. "I don't belong to you."

"Actually, in Zwar, you do."

"People are not objects, Kahlil!"

Pushing the door all the way open, he picked her up, hands encircling her rib cage, thumbs splayed beneath her breasts. His fingers felt like fire against her skin, searing straight through the bodice of her gown. Her breasts tingled, her senses responding to him just as they'd always responded to him. He could turn her into puddles of need in no time flat.

Kahlil tipped her backwards just enough to knock her off her feet, and sent her heart racing. "How could you possibly think I'd let you marry another man? How could you think I'd give you up?"

"Because the divorce—" she choked, beginning to feel genuinely frightened, not by him but by the idea of still being married to him. Their marriage was over; it had to be over.

"What divorce?" he demanded.

"The divorce...our divorce."

The dark hallway threw sinister shadows across his face. "There was no divorce. You never returned the last of the paperwork, and with documents unsigned the divorce was dropped."

Her mouth dried. Her heart hammered harder. She could feel every ragged beat, every quick painful surge of blood. "Documents?" she stuttered, repeating the word as though it were foreign.

"I contested the divorce, refused to accept that you'd left me. It wasn't desertion, I told the judge, but a temporary leave of absence. The judge sent you paperwork and you never filled it out. Therefore the divorce wasn't granted."

"You bought the judge. You gave him money—"

"Don't get carried away. Your legal system isn't all that corrupt. If you want to place blame, place it on your shoulders."

He'd rendered her speechless, stole her breath, her words, her anger.

Could he be possibly right? Had she somehow let paperwork slip?

Her brain raced, struggling to remember that first year, those horrible months of struggling with the baby on her own. She'd moved a half-dozen times in as many months, did temp jobs on top of her regular job just to pay her bills. Swallowing hard Bryn found her voice. "I didn't know you could contest a divorce in Texas."

"In Texas, anything's possible."

She suddenly saw him scooping Ben into his arms, boarding his private jet and taking off. He'd have Ben. She'd never see him again. The vision was so awful, so vivid and real, it felt as though he'd thrust his dagger, the one he wore beneath his robes, straight through her heart. "Why are you doing this?"

His gold-flecked gaze slowly moved across her face, scrutinizing. "You married me. You understand the vows. I'm keeping the vows. And so are you."

"I'll never live with you again, Kahlil."

"But you are my wife. You'll remain my wife."

She crossed her arms over her chest chilled to the bone. A life tied to him. It would be a life in chains. And Ben...she closed her eyes, unable to bear the thought of Ben trapped with her.

Her lashes lifted, her gaze fixed on her husband's face. She'd once found him impossibly beautiful. Now she found him impossibly frightening. "What do you want?"

"You."

Her stomach fell, plummeting to her feet. *Never. Ever, ever.* She dug her fingers into her bare upper arms, fingers pressing into muscle, nails into firm flesh. "It's not going to happen."

He smiled, a small, hard, uncompromising smile. "It will. I'll bet my life on it." Kahlil moved to the door, opened it and stepped onto the small cement porch. "I'll send my car for you tomorrow. We'll have dinner, discuss the future."

She lunged toward him, fists clenched. "There is no future!"

"Oh, yes, there is. How does seven o'clock sound?"

She'd have Ben here then. It would be his bathtime, then stories and bed. She couldn't possibly go out, couldn't possibly let Kahlil return here, either. "You can't just bully your way back into my life. If what you say is true…" Her voice fell away. She swallowed hard, unable to fathom such a truth. After a tense silence she forced herself to continue. "I need time. I need to make some calls, and of course, there is Stan—"

"Oh, yes, nice old Stanley Hopper. Your boss, your fiancé, your insurance agent."

"Get out."

Shrugging he reached for the doorknob, twisting it open. "I'm staying at the Four Seasons. I won't leave town until we've sorted matters out." He leaned over, dropped a kiss on her parted lips. "By the way, you look lovely in that dress."

She'd forgotten all about her wedding gown. Self-consciously she pressed the skirt smooth, the silk delicate and light beneath her fingertips. She'd been trying it on, making sure it didn't need any last-minute alterations. "I wanted to see if it fit."

"It fits." He smiled, eyes glinting. "Beautifully."

Bryn was still shaking an hour after Kahlil finally left. She'd changed, made a cup of tea, but couldn't relax, couldn't calm down.

Kahlil was wrong, he had to be wrong. She wasn't married to him. She wasn't his wife. She *couldn't* be.

Her thoughts raced here, there, scattering in a thousand directions as she drove to Ben's preschool to pick him up.

If she were really still Kahlil's wife, then Kahlil would have a legal right to see Ben. To take Ben.

Making dinner that night Bryn battled to hide her worry from Ben. The cheerful chatter she usually enjoyed grated on her and she was relieved when he finally went to bed and she had some quiet to think.

She paced the small living room, chewing on her thumbnail. The only way she could protect Ben from danger was to keep him a secret, and she didn't know how she'd managed to hide Ben, but she had to. She just had to.

Bryn took the next day off from work and spent it making phone calls—to the courthouse, to lawyers, to anyone who might be able to help her sort out the facts regarding her divorce. With horror she heard one clerk after another explain that paperwork was indeed missing and that the divorce suit had been dropped over a year ago.

Then Kahlil was right. The marriage, *their* marriage, still existed, under Texas law.

It took her another two days to accept the terrible truth. Two days of a churning stomach, and two awful, endless, sleepless nights when she cursed herself for not being on top of details, for failing to ensure the divorce was finalized. This was her fault, her fault entirely.

Finally, heart aching, Bryn called Stan and broke the news. He immediately drove over and they talked for hours but in the end the facts remained the same and there was nothing they could do but postpone the wedding. Stan behaved like a true gentleman, offering no reproaches, just promising his full support.

But after he left, and the house was silent again, Bryn knew she had one last painful phone call to make.

She called the Four Seasons Hotel and was put through to Kahlil's presidential suite. If he sounded surprised to hear from her he gave no indication. But Bryn wasn't about to chitchat. Her voice cool, her tone formal, she suggested they meet the following night for dinner and named a popular Dallas restaurant.

Kahlil offered to send a car, she refused. She'd drive there, she told him, drive home and that would be the last time she'd see him again.

But dinner the next evening didn't start off the way she'd planned. First her car wouldn't start, and then instead of dropping Ben off at the baby-sitter's house, she had to call and ask the sitter to come for Ben. Finally she was forced to phone Kahlil and leave word at the restaurant that she'd be late due to car difficulties. Before the taxi arrived, a black limousine pulled up in front of her house. *Kahlil.* She knew it without a glimpse of him, knew it without a word from him. She felt him. Felt his strength, his anger, his conviction.

From the living-room window she saw him step out of the back and stand next to the limousine's open door. He didn't move. He didn't speak. He simply waited, and in his aggressive stance she saw ownership. He was stating his belief, that she was his, and only his.

Kahlil wasn't going to go away. He wasn't going to leave her alone.

The black limousine sailed on and off the freeway, winding through traffic but Bryn couldn't concentrate on anything. She heard Kahlil say he'd changed their dinner reservation to another restaurant, a quieter one, more conducive to conversation. He said something about taking care of unfinished business but she couldn't think about that, couldn't possibly consider anything between them unfinished. In her mind they were done. Dead. Over.

Not by her choice. It had never been her choice.

The limousine dropped them in front of an exclusive Dallas restaurant, a restaurant requiring membership, and a critical screen before a member could be accepted.

The restaurant entrance was so discreet it looked like a warehouse entrance. However, Bryn found that behind the plain concrete walls and studded steel door, the restaurant walls had been painted in gleaming shades of blue and gold and the gold-leafed ceiling glittered with dozens of extravagant crystal chandeliers.

"Hungry?" Kahlil asked, his hand resting on the small of her back.

She felt every muscle in her tighten, her body snapping to response and Bryn jerked away from him, shocked by her sensitivity. She shouldn't still feel this way. She shouldn't still feel anything. "No."

The maître d' murmured polite greetings, ushering them to a curtained booth. The heavy drapes could be closed, making the table more intimate, if required.

Seated, Bryn's gaze darted to the thick purple drapes, praying they'd remain open, tied back with the gold tasseled ropes. Kahlil ordered drinks for them, and an appetizer. Her hands shook beneath the table. She struggled to breathe normally.

"Smile," he said, leaning back against the plush seat upholstery. "You look like you're being tortured."

"I am being tortured. This is torture."

"How far we've come," he mocked, dark head tipping, black lashes lowering as he studied her grim expression. "Once you would have died for me."

*I almost died living with you.*

But she didn't say it. He knew nothing about her last night in Tiva, or her friendship with his cousin, a friendship that proved to be a terrible, nearly tragic mistake. "You can't take over my life, Kahlil. It's been three years, three and a half years, since we were together. I've changed—"

"Yes, you've grown rebellious."

"I've just grown up. I won't take orders from you anymore."

"I never had to order you to do anything. You did *everything* for me," and his accented voice caressed the word everything, "eagerly."

Her stomach clenched. She wouldn't think about the past, wouldn't think about their old relationship. "Kahlil, I want a divorce and I am going to file for one first thing in the morning. Stan knows an excellent lawyer and he and I *will* be married eventually."

Kahlil made a rude sound, deep in his throat. "I hope your Stan is a patient man because he's going to be kept waiting a very long time. I'll tie you up with every legality I can. You name it, I'll do it."

She stared at him as though he were the devil himself. "Why? What have I ever done to you?"

His golden gaze raked her bare shoulders and simple black dress. "You broke your word."

So that was it. This was just about revenge. About inflicting pain. Fear balled in her stomach and she realized yet again how dangerous this was for Ben.

The appetizer arrived, a savory baked crab dish with buttery crumbs and cheese. Bryn normally loved crab but at the moment her stomach was so queasy she could barely tolerate the smell, much less eat. Kahlil, she noticed, took none, either. "I thought you were famished."

"I am. I'm waiting for you to serve me."

As if she was one of the women from his harem! Incredible. "You are not helpless, Sheikh al-Assad!"

"But why should I serve myself when you are here to serve me?"

She glared at Kahlil, resenting his beauty, the black hair, the strong brow, the elegant sweep of cheekbone. She'd fought so hard to free herself, ripped her heart in two to escape him. It had taken her years to move forward and now that she finally was ready to marry again, he'd returned.

Treacherous man. Man that could disarm her with just a glance from his beautiful eyes. She'd loved him too much, needed more from him than he could give.

Blindly she stumbled to her feet, her long black dress tangling between her legs. His hand snaked around her wrist and drew her roughly down again. "You are not excused." His dark eyes flashed at her, deep grooves etched on either side of his imperious mouth. "You did not ask my permission to leave the table."

"I've never asked your permission for anything and I'm not about to start now!" Good God, who did he think he was? Bryn threw her head back, tears shimmering in her eyes. "I can't believe I once imagined myself in love with you. What a fool I was!"

"You didn't imagine it. You did love me."

"Did," she repeated bitterly, "as in past tense. I only feel hatred for you now."

"Love, hate, who cares? I'm more interested in ensuring you honor your vows." His anger emanated from him in great silent waves. "I realize you were very young when we married but I've given you time to grow up. Three and a half years. Now I've come to bring you home.''

''Zwar is not my home!''

He snapped his fingers. ''Semantics,'' he said brusquely. ''I'm tired of debating. The fact is your place is in Tiva, at the palace, bearing my children.''

''That is one scenario which will *never* happen.''

''You think you'd be happier married to your pathetic little insurance agent? I've had my intelligence look into him and he's a man without fire, a man without drive—''

''And I love him.''

''I don't care. You can't have him.''

Anger swept through her, anger so strong that she lifted her hand and took a swing at his face. He caught her by the wrist just before she struck his cheek. ''Have you lost your mind?''

Her wrist tingled from the tightness of his grip, his fingers wrapped viselike around her fragile bones. ''Leave Stan alone. He doesn't deserve this.''

''But you do. You've insulted me, and my family. You had a responsibility—you were Princess al-Assad— and you abandoned my people.''

Her wrist began to throb. Tiny pinpricks flashed against her closed eyelids. ''Please, release me.''

''I expect an apology.''

''You're hurting me.''

His nostrils flared, his dark eyes flashing, but he opened his fingers, freeing her wrist. She drew her arm back to her lap and stared at her wrist, seeing the livid marks of his fingers against the paleness of her skin.

Kahlil dragged the heavy velvet drapes closed. The violet-purple fabric fell in deep inky folds, hiding them from the rest of the restaurant.

He was pulling her back into his world, forcing her to submit. She couldn't let him. She wasn't just his wife. She was a mother, Ben's mother.

The tears that she'd fought so hard to contain trembled on her lashes, slipping free. She pressed her lips together, fighting to keep control.

"Do not cry," he said roughly. "I won't have my wife weeping in public."

"You've drawn the drapes. No one can see."

"I can see."

Everything about him was so hard. Every word sounded harsh. She clamped her jaw shut, refusing to engage in a battle of wills with Kahlil. He was a far better debater than she. He was far better at everything than she, but that didn't make his needs more important, his feelings more correct.

Kahlil must have accepted her silence for submission as his hard expression gentled a fraction. "If you don't want a fight, don't provoke me. I didn't travel all this way to be scorned by a woman."

Had he always been so arrogant? So damned condescending? Maybe once she'd found his machismo attractive but now it filled her with terror. Terror not just for herself, but Ben, and Ben's future.

If Kahlil knew he had a son, he'd insist that Ben be raised in Zwar, his small oil-rich kingdom in the Middle

East. Zwar was beautiful but far removed from the freedom she and Ben knew in Texas.

Abruptly Kahlil leaned forward, grasped her chin, drawing her toward him. She nearly flinched, inwardly shrinking from his touch, but steeled herself outwardly, not wanting him to know how strongly he affected her.

Yet when he stroked her lips with the pad of his thumb, her whole body shuddered, a response she couldn't possibly hide from Kahlil.

"You've become quite skittish," he drawled, clearly intrigued. "Doesn't Stan ever touch you?"

"My relationship with Stan is none of your business."

"A bold answer for a woman in a precarious position."

Her lips twisted, her smile forced. She ignored the truth in this, realizing she was indeed caught, but pride overwhelmed her common sense. She couldn't back down. "I have changed, Kahlil. I'm not the girl you married."

"Good. Then we both have adjustments to make. I'm not the man you married, either." He smiled without humor, his gaze never wavering from her face. "And you have changed. You've grown more beautiful."

"Don't flatter me."

"I'm not flattering you. I've met a lot of women in my life, but I've never met another woman like you. No one with your sweetness, softness—"

"*Stop.*"

"Your pale, flawless skin. Your eyes, the dark blue of precious sapphires. Your mouth softer than a rose."

Her spine tingled, her skin prickling. *Don't listen to this.* Don't let him get under your skin. You've survived him once. You can do it again. "You only want me because you can't have me."

His fingers opened, freeing her, and his smile remained the same. But his eyes looked harder, the glints brighter. "I can have you. I just haven't been aggressive."

No, he'd never been aggressive with her before tonight, but she suddenly knew he could be extremely ruthless, correctly reading the menace in his hard features, and danger in the crooked curve of his mouth.

His smile faded. "Does Stan know you're a flighty little wife?"

Oh, low blow. "He knows I left you."

"Did you tell him you left without leaving a note? Or giving me a kiss goodbye? He knows you just took your purse, your passport and walked?"

"He knows I took my purse and *ran.*" Her gaze locked with his. If he wanted to make it tough, she could play tough. That's all she'd been doing since leaving Zwar anyway. Cutting coupons to buy breakfast cereal. Shopping for clothes from a secondhand store. Working double shifts at the insurance agency. She'd shouldered parenthood on her own, and succeeded.

"Did Stan ever ask why you left me?"

"He knew I was unhappy, and that was enough for him."

Kahlil lifted his wine goblet, swirled the glass, ruby-red wine shimmering in the candlelight. "What an understanding man. Will he be so understanding when you toss him away, tired of that marriage, too?''

His sarcasm was as sharp as razor blades and cut deep. If she thought she could get away with it, she'd run. But she wouldn't get away from Kahlil, not like that, not this time. ''I never tossed you away.''

''No? It felt that way. It looked that way, too. The palace was wild with gossip. The scandal affected the entire kingdom. I didn't just lose face. My people lost face.''

''What scandal?''

''Rumor has it you were…unfaithful.''

## CHAPTER TWO

*"NEVER."* Color suffused her cheeks, embarrassment and surprise. How could he think such a thing? How could he think the worst?

The realization that he did, hurt far more than she'd expected.

Early on she'd hoped he'd come looking for her. She'd also hoped he'd discover Amin's treachery. Instead Kahlil accepted her betrayal, accepted her failure, accepted that she'd been unfaithful. Apparently it hadn't crossed his mind to even think otherwise.

Then he'd failed her, too. Twice.

Tears burned in her throat, unshed tears she'd never let fall.

Leaving him had nearly destroyed her. It had been the hardest thing she ever had to do. She'd nearly shattered all over again when back in Texas, she discovered she was pregnant.

It was a baby Kahlil wanted. It was a baby he'd never know. The guilt had nearly eaten her alive. Thank God for poverty. It forced her out of bed every morning, forced her to work until she dropped into bed at night, dead with fatigue.

Kahlil might mock Stan and his insurance agency, but working as a secretary at the agency probably saved her life. ''Why don't you just divorce me and get this over with?'' she said hoarsely.

''Can't do that.''

''Why not?'' Lifting her gaze, she looked at Kahlil, noting the firm set of his mouth, the intelligence in his warm golden gaze and saw her son there, the same eyes, the same nose, the same mouth. Why hadn't she ever seen it before? Ben was Kahlil in miniature.

And like that, she saw the awful truth. She and Kahlil weren't completely strangers. They did have something in common, one precious little person. *Ben.*

''Too easy,'' he answered curtly. ''Divorce might be the easiest thing, but I've never taken the easy way out.''

She knew what he was talking about, knew the reference to their marriage. He'd warned her ahead of time that their marriage would create an uproar, predicted his family's reaction, including his father's harsh disapproval. Kahlil had said there would be hell to pay and she'd shrugged it off, kissing Kahlil's lovely mouth, his cheekbone, his jaw. She'd been confident she could win his family over, so certain that Kahlil's love and approval would be enough.

And she was wrong. Very wrong.

Knots balled along her shoulder blades, her back rigid, her neck stiff. Her gaze settled on his hard profile. Once she'd love to kiss the strong angles and planes of his face. She remembered how she lavished extra kisses on the small scar near the bridge of his nose.

She could feel the heartbreak again, thick and sharp. She had loved him. Once. She'd wanted nothing but to be with him. She loved him to distraction, needed the assurance he felt the same. Instead he withdrew, his warmth disappearing behind an impersonal mask. Duty, country, business. Their worlds no longer connected, their lives ceased to touch.

"How badly do you want a divorce?"

His question sent small shock waves rippling through her middle. He was toying with her the same cruel way a cat played with a mouse just before the mouse became a feline supper.

Her spine stiff, her shoulders squared, she lifted her chin, wanting to defy him. She wouldn't dignify his games with an answer. Let him speak first. Let him be the one to grope for explanations.

But her righteous anger collapsed on itself, even as she confronted the enormity of her problem. This wasn't a small matter. Ben's whole future was at stake. Rather than provoking Kahlil, she needed to work with him, humor him. The baby-sitter, Mrs. Taylor, would be dropping Ben off at eleven, less than three hours from now. She needed to be home by then, and she had to be rid of Kahlil by then. "Badly," she choked.

"Badly enough to risk everything?"

"What do you mean by everything?"

"You'd become mine for the weekend."

She reached for her water glass, lifted it to her mouth. The rim of the chilled glass clicked against her teeth, icy water sloshing against her lips.

He leaned forward. "I want you for a weekend."

"That's your proposal?"

"I'm giving you an opportunity to take control of your life."

"I spend a weekend with you, and you'd grant me a divorce?"

"If my terms were met."

He made it sound so easy. Bryn stared at the water drops darkening the white cloth, her mind strangely blank. No words, no sound, no light filtering through her brain. "And those terms…?"

"I want a long weekend with you. Four days. Three nights. City of my choosing."

She touched one of the damp drops on the tablecloth with her finger. "You want me to be your wife."

"I want you to be my lover."

Her head lifted, gaze meeting his. He smiled without a hint of warmth in the eyes. "I want to possess you, enjoy you at my leisure, and make you mine—completely mine—again."

Something inside her stirred, hunger, awareness. He knew how she responded to him. He knew he could seduce her at the drop of the hat. "You don't think I have the strength to walk away from you a second time."

He shrugged. "Did I say that?"

"You don't have to. I know you."

"If you please me, I shall process the divorce papers in Zwar. If you cannot fulfill the required duties to my satisfaction, you shall return to Zwar with me and take lessons from the palace concubines."

"Either way, you win."

He ignored that. "You'd only sacrifice four days of your life, and surely, Stan's love is worth at least that?"

Stan's love was worth more, but Kahlil's price...

Four days in his bed. Four days making love. A vision of tangled limbs, warm bodies, damp skin flashed before her and she felt blood race to her cheeks. "It's a humiliating proposition."

"But it gives you possibilities. Hopes for the future."

Hopes for the future. Ben's future.

Bryn draw a deep breath, and actually considered his offer. Just for a moment. Alone, naked, weak. He'd reduce her to hunger and fire all over again and she would need him too much, want him too much. Like before.

It was too risky. For herself, and for Ben. She felt raw, exposed, Kahlil's proposal peeling off needed protective layers that shielded her heart from the past, and the danger Kahlil still posed.

Something wonderful and awful happened when they were together. She felt more alive, more physical, more aware, but that acute awareness came at a terrible price. Kahlil made her feel emotions and desires that she couldn't control. It hurt then, it hurt now, and this feeling couldn't be natural or normal. Emotions shouldn't run so deep.

"I can't," she gasped, dying inside. "There's just no way."

His mouth curved, a crooked smile. "You don't have to give me your answer yet. You might want to think it over a little longer. Take an hour. Take two. After all, it is your future."

Dinner finished, Kahlil tossed a handful of bills on the table—several hundred dollars, Bryn noted woodenly, chump change to Kahlil and a small fortune to herself. Money like that would pay for new shoes for Ben. A rib roast for Sunday supper. Maybe even a night on the Gulf Coast.

Resentful tears pricked the back of her eyes as Kahlil steered her to his waiting limousine. He had no idea what it was like to struggle and worry about every purchase, every trip to the grocery store, every new month because it meant starting the vicious cycle over again— rent, gas, electric bill, car payment, and on and on until Bryn wanted to scream. It hadn't helped that Stan was always offering to ease her load, make payments for her, pick up expenses. She'd been sorely tempted but had never accepted his offers, never accepted his frequent marriage proposals, either—not until last Christmas.

She'd finally worn down resisting, reluctantly accepting that bald, bespectacled Stanley would be the right thing. Not for her. But for Ben.

Numbly Bryn slid into the back of the limousine and buckled her seat belt across her lap.

Kahlil directed the driver back to her house.

Bryn's fog of misery lifted, recognizing the peril of letting Kahlil close to her home. Ben's toys and bedroom had been packed for the move but there could be knick-knacks around the house, photos or artwork she'd overlooked. ''Why don't we go for a drive?''

''A drive?''

She ignored Kahlil's incredulity. ''Or a walk. It's a

beautiful night. Not too humid for the first time in weeks.''

Kahlil viewed her through narrowed lashes, his expression speculative. ''Who are we hiding from?''

The fact that he could read her so easily reinforced her fear, as well as her determination to be rid of him as soon as possible. Already she felt as though she was drowning, the water rising, destruction imminent. She had the agonizing suspicion that she might not be able to pull this off. Kahlil was so clever, too clever, and also too angry.

No sooner had she swallowed the sour taste of panic than she pictured Ben as he'd run out of the house earlier, eager to go with Mrs. Taylor. His small white sneakers had slapped the sidewalk, his miniature jeans rolled up at the ankle. She always bought his clothes big, trying to make them last two seasons, maybe even three.

He'd stopped at Mrs. Taylor's truck, turned around to wave and he blew her an enormous kiss. ''I love you, Mommy!''

His zest brought tears to her eyes and laughing, she'd blown him a kiss back. She'd felt a spike of worry then, the kind of worry she felt every time she kissed him good-night, what if something happened? What if there was an accident? What if she lost him? What if…

The what-ifs could drive her crazy.

Fierce love rose up within her, love, determination and conviction. She wouldn't fail Ben. She'd fight tooth and nail to protect him. He was the one perfect and true thing she'd ever known.

Bryn looked at Kahlil, gaze level, mouth smiling faintly. "Is there something criminal in wanting to walk?"

"You never liked to walk before."

"Of course not. I was eighteen. I preferred motorbikes and race cars and anything else that jolted my heart." Like you, she thought cynically. You jolted my heart a thousand times a day.

Kahlil gave the driver directions to a popular downtown park, the night quiet, the streets nearly deserted. The limousine pulled over to the curb and Kahlil and Bryn got out, to stoically circle the square.

The evening, balmy for late September, smelled sweeter than usual, the peculiar ripe fragrance of turning leaves as summer slipped away, fading into fall.

He didn't speak. She didn't try, chewing her lower lip, struggling to come up with an alternative to Kahlil's proposal, one that might meet his need for vengeance without endangering Ben. But no solutions came to mind, immediately dismissing lawsuits and threats, as well as fleeing with Ben. This time Kahlil wouldn't let her go. He'd find her, and he'd really want blood then.

They passed the fountain and large bronze statue twice with Bryn still overwhelmed with worry.

Kahlil thrust his hands into his trouser pockets. "There's no way out," he said mildly, casting a curious side glance her way. "You're not going to escape without settling the score."

A flurry of nerves made her prickle from head to toe. How could he know exactly what she was thinking? "Score. Proposition. You're trying to humiliate me."

"Clever girl." He stopped walking, facing her, his dark features mocking. "You humiliated me before my family and my people. You're fortunate that your humiliation will be much more…private."

"What makes you think I'd agree to this plan?"

"You were once quite daring. You hungered for adventure, for travel and the unknown. Is the great unknown no longer appealing?"

No. Not since becoming a mother. She worried constantly about Ben. His safety, his security, his future. And since becoming a mother, she wondered how her own parents could have dragged her through the Middle East as a small child, living out of tents and the camper van, sleeping at desolate spots along the road. They'd led a precarious life and it had cost them all. Dearly.

Pain suffused her, time and grief blurring her parents' faces. She remembered them better by photograph than be special memories. "I prefer things simple now," she answered faintly. "My relationships uncomplicated."

"Like Stan?"

Her eyes flashed warning. "Leave him out of this."

"How can I? He's the enemy."

"Stan is not the enemy. *You're* the enemy."

He laughed, the husky sound carrying in the darkness. "Four days. Four days and you'd be free. You could marry Stan. Have a family. Get on with your life."

Oh, how like Kahlil, how clever, how manipulative. Trust the devil to suggest temptation.

But the devil knew her, she acknowledged weakly. He knew how she'd reached for him, again and again, undone by the pleasure of their bodies, so inexperienced that she couldn't be satiated, her untutored desires wanting more.

But that wasn't the kind of relationship she had with Stan. Her fault, she knew, but despite her gratitude to Stan, she didn't enjoy it when he touched her. She told herself that her feelings would change after their wedding, but would they? Could they?

Warily she glanced at Kahlil. Moonlight illuminated his profile. If she did go with him, if she did all that he asked, would he really set her free? Could she trust him to honor his word?

"You can't pick the city," she said, feeling trapped, the air squeezing out of her lungs. She wouldn't breathe until she was free of him. "Four days, three nights. I pick the place, the city and the hotel."

"The city and the hotel? Now you're sounding paranoid."

She refused to be baited, too busy examining the proposal from every angle. A couple of nights with him in New York. How bad could it be? She'd do what he asked and then she'd have her divorce. "New York," she said. "The Ritz-Carlton Hotel."

"Paris. The Ritz-Carlton."

"I won't leave the States."

"You don't trust me?"

"No." She lifted her chin. "As it is you act as judge, jury and executioner. It hardly seems fair."

He laughed without kindness. "I guess you'd have to work very very hard at pleasing me."

Seething, she returned to the limousine, realizing she was only wasting time—his, hers and Ben's. Kahlil might look like a modern man with his expensive clothes and gorgeous face, but his thinking was still feudal.

The limousine drew to a stop before her house and Kahlil's driver opened the back door. But before she could move, Kahlil clasped her elbow.

"It might not be safe going with me," he said softly, "but it might also be the smartest thing you've ever done. Everything in life is a risk. Even your freedom."

She didn't speak. She couldn't.

Lightly he stroked her bare arm, his touch sending shock waves through her body. "The weekend wouldn't be without its rewards," he continued. "You burn for me. You're on fire now."

She stared at her arm in mute fascination. She did feel feverish, her skin blazing, her body melting, everything in her coming alive in response to him. He'd always made her feel like this, crazy with need. Right now her nerves throbbed, her pulse racing. He was a drug, sweetly addictive, dangerously destructive, utterly transforming. In his bed, in his arms, she would do anything for him.

Leave her home, change her name, worship at his feet. She lost control when it came to him and that loss of control completely shamed her.

She breathed deeply, dizzy, torn between wildly opposing desires. Run. Stay. Scream. Kiss.

If she went with him, she'd enjoy Kahlil's revenge. She'd welcome the humiliation as it would be at his hands, in his hands, with his body.

A woman should have more self-respect. She had none.

She could feel the press of his thigh against hers, his hips close, his warmth stealing into her. He promised intense sensual pleasure, a pleasure she'd only ever known with him.

Color banded in high hot waves across her cheek-bones. Closing her eyes, she swayed, drawn to him.

He held her in his power again.

*Stop it.*

*Wake up. You can't do this. Think about Ben. Think about the dangers in the palace. At the very least, think about Amin.*

Her eyes opened, her lips parted, and reality returned. ''I can't do it, Kahlil. I won't. We need to make a clean break of it.'' Was that her voice? High? Thin? Panicked?''

''Clean break,'' he mocked. ''Hardly, darling. You'd remain my wife.''

''That's not fair!''

''Life's not fair.''

She averted her face, struggling to hide the tumultuous emotions from him. She was angry, aroused, torn. If she didn't go away with him, Kahlil would discover Ben.

But spending a weekend with Kahlil was like throwing herself in the mouth of a volcano.

It was Ben's future, or hers.

Ben's or hers.

Ben won. "No other man would force a woman to submit," she said bitterly, unable to hide her anger or despair. He'd never planned on releasing her from their marriage vows. He'd given her time but not forgiveness. Space but not freedom. And without a divorce she could permanently lose Ben.

Kahlil didn't answer. He didn't need to. They both knew he wasn't just any man. He was a sheikh, his word in his country was law.

Eyes gritty and hot, she drew a short breath. "God, I hate you."

"I don't care. I want what's mine. And you, wife, are mine."

He was going to kiss her. She knew it, felt it, just before his head dropped. Alarm shrieked through her, alarm because in his arms she was weak, so weak, it made her sick.

She tried to slip away but Kahlil moved even faster. He blocked the door and leveraged her backward, her spine pressed to the leather seat. "You can't escape me," he murmured, his voice husky as his palm slid down her throat, spanning the column, forming a collar with his hand. "But then, I don't think you really want to." And with that, his head dropped, his mouth covering hers.

His warmth caught her unawares, his skin fragrant, a

soft subtle sweet spice she couldn't place, but a fragrance that had been part of him as long as she'd known him. The very first time they'd touched she'd breathed him in, again and again, heart racing, spectacular colors and visions filling her head. She saw the full white moon above the bleached ivory sands, the grove of orange trees planted within the village walls, the warmth of the night in the darkest hour…

Kahlil.

Her lashes closed, lips parting beneath the pressure of his, welcoming him, the sweetness and the strength, the memory of their lives. She'd loved him, oh God, she'd loved him, and he'd filled her, capturing her heart and mind and soul.

Kahlil.

His tongue traced the inside of her lip, sending rivulets of feeling in her mouth, her belly, between her thighs. She tensed at the quicksilver sensation, the warmth, first hot then turning icy as he flicked his tongue across her lip again.

Helplessly she clasped his shirt, holding on to him tightly as shudders coursed down her spine. He felt so familiar, wonderfully warm, hard, real. For months she'd wept at night missing him, missing his skin, his scent, his passion for her, for their brief bittersweet year together.

The shiny green leaf of citrus, the spice of cardamom, the tangy essence of lemon…Kahlil…and her body warmed, softening for him, responding, ignoring the revolt of her mind, refusing to remember anyone or anything but the pleasure of being in his arms.

His hand slid from her throat to her breast, his touch igniting fire beneath her skin. Shuddering, she curved more closely against him, seeking more contact, more of his strength.

"Tell me," his voice rasped, "is this how you respond to Stan, too?"

Bryn felt ice invade her limbs. Stiffening in horror, she pushed frantically at his chest, desperate to escape.

Kahlil laughed deep in his throat. "Oh, don't stop making love to me, darling. I'm really rather aroused."

Disgust, remorse, hurt shot through her like sharp arrows, piercing her conscience, reminding her who Kahlil really was. A savage. A savage from a savage land. Hurt turned to anger, the emotion blistering, and her arm swung up, fingers flexing, palm wide. She caught him square on the cheek, the slap echoing shockingly loud in the silent car.

He didn't move, but she could hear the ring of her hand against his cheek, hear it play again and again in her head. My God, what had she done? How could she have hit him of all people? "I'm sorry."

He didn't speak and she sat frozen on the seat, fingers pressed to her mouth, eyes wide with shock. Sick at heart, she stared at his cheek, seeing through the shadows the reddened area of his skin.

"Twice tonight you've lifted your hand against me, once you actually made contact." He spoke without a hint of emotion in his husky voice. "This is not a good habit."

She ought to apologize again but couldn't speak, too many powerful emotions swirling within her. She wanted him and hated him. Craved his touch yet longed to wound him. It was madness. Being near him was madness. How could she ever escape him again?

"This habit must be quickly broken. Do you understand, Princess al-Assad?"

"Don't call me Princess. I'm not a princess."

"But you are. And as long as you are my wife, you are entitled to my name, my fortune, my protection."

"No—"

"You can't escape it. Marrying me has changed your life." His gaze found hers, light and shadow playing across his granitelike features, even as he stepped from the car, and taking her hand in his, drew her out after him. "Forever."

# CHAPTER THREE

THE phone was ringing inside the house. Bryn could hear it from the walkway and climbed the porch steps quickly, struggling to get the house key into the lock, but her hands shook so badly she couldn't connect.

"Need help?" Kahlil drawled, a taunt in his voice.

"*No.*"

The phone continued to ring, the persistence of the caller creating fresh worry. What if it was Mrs. Taylor? What if something happened to Ben? Anxiously she jammed the key into the dead bolt and gave it a fierce turn. The lock gave way and she stepped inside even as the phone stopped ringing.

Kahlil must have heard the frustration in her sigh because as he brushed past her, he touched the tip of her nose with his finger. "If it's important, love, he'll call back."

Kahlil left her to wander the house, moving from the narrow dark hall into her tiny kitchen. It infuriated her that he walked right in without invitation. She followed him into the kitchen where he sucked up air and space, reducing the cramped area to nothing more than a shoebox.

Spine rigid, Bryn watched his critical gaze examine the chipped painted cupboards and worn beige linoleum.

She could tell he'd missed nothing, not even the limp dish towels hanging from the chrome bar.

"If you needed cash, you should have told me," he said at last, turning to face her, arms crossed over his chest. His folded arms accented the width of his shoulders, the tug of fabric outlined his strong biceps. Kahlil had always been built big, all hard, carved muscle, imposing even by American standards.

She drew a short, sharp breath, her head hurting, her heart hurting again. She wouldn't let him do this, wouldn't let his wealth change her feelings. This house had been home to every good memory of her life with Ben. All those wonderful firsts…his first smile, first tooth, first step, first word. Baby powder and lullabies. Mashed peas and sweet gummy kisses. A cocoon she'd spun around them, safe, fragile, wonderful. Their world had sustained her. Until now.

"I don't need your money." She choked. "I like my home. It's cozy."

"Cozy's quaint. This is decrepit."

She pressed her lips together, fighting tears of shame. Of course he'd sneer at her secondhand furniture. In Sheikh al-Assad's world, everything was the best. The best cars. The best furniture. The best jewelry. But she couldn't afford luxuries. She could barely pay her rent every month. But Ben was healthy and happy and she wouldn't trade his security for all the luxuries in the world. "I never asked you in. If you're not comfortable, see yourself out. You know where the door is."

"And what? Deprive myself of you? Oh, no, I'm staying.'' He leaned against one laminated counter, relaxed, smiling. ''However, for a Southerner, your hospitality is shocking. The proper thing would be to offer your guest some refreshment.''

She had an hour left to get rid of him, an hour before Mrs. Taylor returned with Ben. ''It's late, Kahlil.''

''Yes, and a cup of coffee would be lovely. Thank you.''

Her head began to ache, a low throbbing pain that dulled her senses. What point was there in arguing with him? He was deaf when he wanted to be, blind when he found it convenient. Which is what had drove them apart in Tiva. Kahlil immersed in palace affairs. Bryn lost and alone. She'd tried talking to him then, but he hadn't heard her, just as he wasn't listening now.

Wearily she put the kettle on the stove, still making coffee the way Kahlil had taught her, French-press style, stronger, darker, richer than American brewed coffee. Some habits, she noted dryly, were hard to break.

''As *cozy* as you find your house, I think we could do better for you.'' Kahlil's voice, emotionless, echoed in the close quarters. ''You need something more appropriate for your position. I'll hire you a housekeeper. A driver. Bodyguards.''

She didn't even turn around. ''I don't need bodyguards, or a driver. And I may be poor but I'm an excellent housekeeper. You won't find a bit of dust anywhere.''

''Just wanted to make things easier for you.''

"A divorce would make things easier. A housekeeper would merely be a nuisance."

"Don't think about the money—"

"I'm not," she interrupted curtly, gripping the quilted potholder between her hands. She was thinking of Ben, worrying about him, seeing the danger she'd unwittingly thrust him in. "You can't do this. You can't take over my life."

"I have valid concerns about your safety."

Just then the telephone rang again. Bryn tensed, shoulders knotting. Her skin prickled with dread. She didn't want to answer the phone, but couldn't ignore it, either.

Kahlil read her indecision. "Let it ring," he commanded, authoritative as ever. "It doesn't concern us."

Even from where he stood, she could feel him, catch a whiff of his cologne. Musky, rich, reminiscent of the East with cardamom, citrus, spice. It made her picture him naked in the silk sheets of his opulent bed, bronze skin covering sinewy muscle. He was built like a god. He made love like a god. She'd worshiped him.

Then he fell from the pedestal and nothing had ever been the same between them again, leaving her vulnerable to Amin's dangerous games.

The phone rang again. Four times. Five.

She moved to answer it but Kahlil stopped her, his hands coming down to rest on her shoulders. "Leave the phone. Listen to what I'm saying."

"I can't—"

"You can. You must. You've kept me waiting three

years. I think you owe me five minutes of your undivided attention.''

But she was listening to the phone, silently counting the rings. Five, six, seven. "Please, Kahlil.''

"No.''

She closed her eyes, her body trembling, her heart barely beating. Eight, nine. And then it stopped. The phone went dead.

Brilliant red-hot pain consumed her even as she had a terrifying vision of the future, a future far from her home in Texas, a future of blistering sands and dark veils covering her from head to toe.

"You do not own me, Sheikh al-Assad, and you will not put me in another prison!'' she raged, her fury not just at him, but against his family, his customs, his inability to see her as anything but an extension of him.

"The palace was never a prison!''

"It felt like one. You left me there alone, trapped in the harem.''

"You knew in advance the wives eat, sleep, socialize in their own quarters. You were raised in the Middle East. You knew our customs.''

"But I married *you*. I expected to be with *you*.''

"And you were, at night. I had you brought to me most evenings, if I wasn't away on business, or obligated to entertain.'' He drew a deep breath, his composure also shaken. He pressed knuckles to his temple, his jaw rock-hard. "Regardless of your feelings about the palace, we can't afford to take chances with your safety. The problem with being a princess worth millions—billions of dollars—is that people will come at you from every direction.''

''No one even knows I'm your wife!''

''They will.''

The assurance in his voice sent shivers down her spine. They will because he'd make sure people knew she belonged to him, he'd make sure no one like Stan could ever grow fond of her, make sure she remained alone in the ivory tower. ''You'll make me a prisoner in my own home.''

''The price we pay for being rich.''

Tears filled her eyes, and she averted her head.

''Your parents were killed by extremists,'' he continued more softly. ''You, of all people, should know that the world is dangerous.''

''And I've chosen to live without fear.'' Once she left Zwar she turned her back on exotic locales and wild adventure. No more nomadic travels. No more yearning for far-off places. Her parents' instability had destroyed their family. She wouldn't do that to Ben.

''I will not become someone else just to give you peace of mind,'' she added hoarsely, unwilling to remember the bomb blast at the marketplace or the horror of her parents' death. She'd been sent to Aunt Rose in Dallas, and Rose had been wonderful. Thank God for her aunt's warmth and support.

She felt rather than heard Kahlil move behind her. He walked quietly, stealthily, like a big cat. Beautiful and oh, so lethal.

"And I will not let a hair on your head be harmed," he murmured, reaching out and drawing her toward him.

She tensed and he kissed the back of her neck.

His lips against her skin, and it was the most amazing pleasure she could imagine.

A shudder raced through her, nipples hardening, heat filling her belly. Just a kiss and she wanted him. Just a touch and she started to melt.

Her nerves screamed. Hot tears stung her closed eyes. She wanted to feel his hand on her breasts, her stomach, her thighs.

Slowly he plucked the tortoiseshell pins from her coiled hair, combing the long tangled strands smooth. "Not a hair," he repeated, lifting the light gold strands, fingers caressing the silky length. "Despite everything, I still want you, I still want to love your body."

*"No."* It was a desperate denial, her lips twisting as shudders of feeling traveled the length of her spine. She felt warm where she'd been cold. Soft where she ought to be hard. *Resist him. Resist him!*

"Yes. And I forgive you," he added, kissing her nape again, creating fresh pleasure, more intense sensation. His hands slid to her shoulders. He held her securely. "I forgive you and want only to have you home again."

His words cut her, deep stabbing wounds, reminding her of the secret she'd worked so hard to keep from him. She'd spent the last three years denying she'd ever been part of him, ignoring that her child, their child...

But his home would never be her home, not after what Amin had done. Not after what she had done.

Kahlil's lips moved across her nape and Bryn closed her eyes, head falling forward, caught up in the rawness of her emotions. Need flamed inside her, need to be held, touched, loved. Stan cared for her but it had never felt like this. Never had the power, or the passion.

The old kettle began to boil, the little cap whistling softly. "We have to move on," she choked, the air aching inside her lungs, her heart as fragile as a delicate glass ornament. Remembering the damage Amin had done, Kahlil would never forgive her betrayal, never understood why she turned to his cousin. "I need to put the past behind. I need to go forward."

The teakettle's whistle grew louder. "But I cannot."

"Why not? You're one of the most accomplished, educated men in the Middle East. You hold degrees from Oxford and Harvard—"

He reached past her, moved the kettle from the burner, silencing the shrill whistle. "I might have been educated in the West, but my pride, is Arabic. I am Arabic. And my pride demands justice. An eye for an eye…a tooth for a tooth…"

"A humiliation for a humiliation," she added, turning slowly, helplessly, toward him.

"Exactly."

"So until I go with you on this weekend, I will never be free."

He didn't say anything. He didn't have to.

Kahlil watched her eyes widen, the blue irises flecked with bright bits of purple and black. Anger and defiance burned in her eyes, turning the color to glowing sapphires, rich, rare, prized.

"You aren't really giving me a choice then, are you?" she demanded.

He checked the smile that curled the corners of his mouth. She looked the picture of injured innocence, eyes bright, full soft lips trembling. Oh, but didn't he know that expression? And hadn't he heard that same inflection play through his head at least a thousand times since the night she'd left him?

He found it ironic, too, that even angry, she was still prettier than a poster girl, her face all heart-shaped sweetness, her creamy skin framed by silky hair the color of citron and sunshine. He had always loved her hair, loved to run his hands through the softness and the hundred different shades of gold spill through his fingers.

He'd been furious when Amin told him about Bryn's wedding. He couldn't believe she dared to marry another man. His anger burned so hotly that he'd feared what he'd do when he arrived at her house, but when she opened the door, the violence in his heart faded, leaving only resolve. She was his. She would go home with him.

"Of course you have a choice. You can be mine, completely, for four nights, or you can be mine, in name, for the rest of your life. It's entirely up to you."

The choice obviously horrified her, and for a moment he felt almost sympathy, until he remembered how she'd walked out on him, no apology, no attempt to reconcile, nothing. She vowed to love him and she broke that vow, in less than a year.

It was time she learned the importance of a promise. In Zwar, one's life depended on one's word.

She moved away from him, filling the French press with boiling water, tightening the top, pushing the coffee through the fine grounds. He watched her hands, watched the concentration on her face.

She handed him his cup, careful to avoid touching him. "How did you know I was getting married?"

"Amin told me." He lifted his cup to his mouth, sipped the strong black liquid, noting the flicker in her eyes and the sudden press of her lips. "Your hatred for my cousin is unacceptable, and undeserved. No one has supported you more than he."

"I can imagine."

"You doubt me?"

"I doubt him." Her voice was as brittle as a branch encased in ice. "How did he find out about the wedding?"

Kahlil shrugged. "He spotted your announcement on the Internet while reading a Dallas paper."

"Don't you find that rather coincidental? Amin reading a Dallas newspaper on the Internet? Why should he care about Dallas news?"

"I have investments here. Manufacturers. Oil refineries." He watched her struggle to control her temper and he frowned. "You scorn his loyalty, but he's been more faithful than you, my young wife."

It was on the tip of her tongue to indict Amin, to blurt

the terrible truth about Kahlil's favorite cousin, but before she could speak she heard a car pull up outside, parking next to her house.

Goose bumps peppered her flesh. It couldn't be Mrs. Taylor back already, could it?

She was moving for the door, practically running. She heard Kahlil speak, something about her decision and had she made a choice, but she didn't answer, dread, fear, panic consuming her.

From the front door Bryn caught a glimpse of a truck parked at her curb. Mrs. Taylor's old Ford pickup. And next to Mrs. Taylor she spotted a small dark head. Ben.

That was the phone call. Mrs. Taylor had been ringing to let Bryn know she'd be returning Ben early. And here she was, bringing Benjamin home at the absolute worst possible time, straight into the arms of his father.

''Friends?'' Kahlil asked, appearing behind her. She couldn't see his face but she felt his tension, his gaze focused on the truck parked outside and the passengers within.

She couldn't have answered him if her life depended on it.

The truck door opened and a child tumbled out dressed in jeans, T-shirt, white sneakers.

She couldn't help it, couldn't stay in place. She was out the door and down the front steps, running toward the truck, her eyes only on Ben. Her heart felt like a mashed plum, pulpy and bruised. As she reached her son, swinging him up into her arms, she knew she'd lost.

She couldn't do anything right. Couldn't even protect Ben when she needed to most.

Cold from head to toe, Bryn began to tremble. Her arms felt like matchsticks. Her legs like feather pillows. Sinking to the ground, she collapsed onto the rough asphalt. It was over. The hiding, the running, the pretending. It was over.

She hugged Ben hard, needing him, fearing for him. Every choice in her life, every mistake she'd made, had come to this.

Kahlil's footsteps sounded behind her. The leather heels of his shoes echoing too loudly on the cracked cement walk.

Bryn closed her eyes, praying for a miracle, praying that somehow she could disappear with Ben, prevent this terrible moment from happening. Instead Kahlil came to a standstill beside her, towering above them, the legs of his dark trousers just inches from her bent head.

''Would you care to explain?'' Kahlil asked quietly, his accent pronounced, his English formal, just the way they'd taught him in boarding school.

Her stomach heaved. Her teeth began to chatter.

But Ben, so young, so innocent, lifted his dark head, and stared at Kahlil, wide brown eyes fixed intently on his father's angry face. ''Mommy, who is that man?''

# CHAPTER FOUR

WITHIN minutes of boarding the Learjet, the engines roared to life and they were off, taxiing down the runway, lifting from the ground. The sparkling lights of Texas fell away, and the night ominously purple-black, stretched silently before them.

Bryn wrapped her arms more snugly around Ben, her nerves close to breaking. She was grateful he finally slept, his thousand questions during the drive to the airport so innocent and yet so troubling. *Where are we going, Mommy? Will we stay at a hotel? Can we go swimming?*

Can we go swimming?

Oh God, what a question! For him this was an adventure, an exciting break from the day-to-day. He was with his mommy, he was on an airplane, and he'd been given a glass of soda pop. What else could a three-year-old want?

She closed her eyes, a lump sealing her throat, tears not far off. Everything she'd fought for the last three years had been lost. Ben's safety was now in question. It all depended on Kahlil.

And Kahlil had said nothing since they boarded his plane two hours ago. But she knew him well enough to read his mood, his hard features set in sharp, tight lines,

51

his temper barely leashed. Oh, he was angry. No, he was more than angry, he was livid.

She swallowed hard, swallowing around the lump, feeling as though she was choking, fear, panic, regret knotting inside her, making her completely crazed.

What would happen now? What would Kahlil do?

Ben stirred fretfully, protesting her tense grip. More gently she shifted him, slowly rocking in the leather lounge chair.

Ben relaxed again, his small body curling more closely against her, his soft cheek settling against her breast.

She felt his breath, and his shudder, as he sighed in his sleep. Her heart ached, her love for him almost too painful, too intense. Had her parents felt this way about her? And if so, why hadn't she known it?

She'd been without her parents now nearly as many years as she'd spent with them and their memory was blurring, not their faces as they appeared in photographs, but their voices, the inflections, the conversations they'd had with her. She remembered their love for their work, their passion for the desert and the nomadic people of the Middle East, but she couldn't recall the things they'd said to her, the little things about her interests, her needs, her dreams.

But it wasn't her needs that were important now, it was Ben. *His* interests. His needs. And she vowed now, as she had since his birth, that he'd have security. He'd be safe. He'd feel loved.

She pressed another kiss to the top of his warm brow

before smoothing a fistful of black hair back from his flushed face. He was beautiful, jet-black hair, dark eyes, perfectly made. So much like Kahlil...

"When is his birthday, Bryn?"

Kahlil knew. It was obvious Ben was his. They shared the same eyes, nose, beautiful curve of cheek and jaw. Even though Ben was young you could see the hints of the man he'd be.

Hot tears scalded her eyes. "May 8."

Kahlil didn't speak. He didn't need to. She could feel his swift mental calculations and he added it up for himself, their wedding, the months between, the birth of Ben. She'd conceived him after their honeymoon when all she wanted was to be alone and naked with Kahlil, skin on skin, fingers and lips, bodies and hunger. She'd wanted him, all of him, with passion and desperation, her heart awakening, her senses stirred. She'd never felt so alive.

"My son," Kahlil said flatly, gaze hooded, lips pressed into a fierce line.

"Yes."

Kahlil rose from his leather armchair and crossed the cabin, moving to a small table between them. He selected a piece of dried fruit from the silver tray. "You," he said quietly, "have made a terrible mistake."

Venom filled his voice. He would make her suffer.

"So silent, Princess al-Assad. An evening of protests and now silence."

She couldn't tear her gaze from the apricot in his fingers. He was squeezing it, flattening it in the press of his fingers, just as he longed to mash her, force her to submit. With an effort she dragged her gaze from the fruit to his face. "I'm sorry."

He popped the apricot into his mouth, chewing it slowly, swallowing after a long moment. "You are only sorry you were caught."

She wondered at the truth in that. Was that the only reason she felt such overwhelming sorrow?

Again she thought of her parents, their love for each other, their love for their work, very little room for her. Had she kept Ben from Kahlil out of selfishness? Had she kept Ben a secret to ensure she had someone of her own to love?

But a choice like that, selfish, blind, would have only hurt Ben. "No. That's not true," she said, forcing herself to speak. "Everything I've done has been done to protect Ben."

"You think I'd hurt my son?" Kahlil's tone was so cold it cut. "Is that the kind of man you think I am?"

No, but he was blind, at least when it came to his cousin. Kahlil favored Amin. Always had, always would.

Ben could be hurt by Amin. If Amin would attack her, why would Ben be exempt?

"Your silence speaks volumes," Kahlil said cuttingly, fresh contempt in his voice and the hard lines of his face. His features were perfectly imperial—strong high forehead, long, straight nose, firm mouth with just a hint of sensuality and a square, stubborn chin.

"I was thinking of Ben," she answered softly, drawing him closer. "Everything is changing for him."

"As it should."

"He'll be frightened."

"He'll be fine. He has me now."

Kahlil wouldn't remove her from Ben's life, would he? He wouldn't hurt her—or Ben—like that, would he?

Brilliant pain streaked through her, her breath catching as tears burned her eyes. "I'll do anything you ask, just be gentle with him. He's still so young—"

"I can see that for myself. I can see his devotion to you, too. I would not hurt him, Bryn. I would not wound my own flesh."

She bowed her head, struggling to contain the swell of emotion. "We're going to Zwar then?"

"We should land in Tiva in six hours."

And Amin? Was he there? Would he be waiting? "Your family…do they know I'm coming?"

"My father's dead," Kkalil said shortly. "He died almost two years ago."

"I'm sorry. I didn't know."

"You don't read newspapers?"

She tried to avoid any mention of Zwar, tried to barricade her from her old life with Kahlil. "I'm sorry," she repeated helplessly.

"My cousin, Mala, the one that was about your age, she's in London now, finishing graduate school. So she won't be there. The rest are scattered."

"And Amin?"

Kahlil shot her a quick, hard glance. ''He lives abroad. Prefers Monte Carlo's nightlife to Tiva.''

Relief swept through her, wave after wave of the sweetest news she'd heard in days.

Kahlil poured himself a drink. ''Want one?'' he asked, lifting the liqueur decanter.

''No. Thank you.''

The golden liquid gleamed in the brandy glass. ''Tell me about my son.''

That's right. Kahlil was a stranger to Ben. She felt a pang of remorse. It was a terrible thing to do to him. But had there been a choice? Was there another option she hadn't thought of?

''I'd like to know him,'' Kahlil added softly, his features tightening, his expression bleak.

The pang of remorse grew, widening to grief. ''Ben is three going on eighty,'' she said carefully. ''He's what I call an old soul. One of those children that are born knowing everything already. He's very gentle, very loving. There isn't a mean bone in his body.''

''What does he like to play?''

''Cars, trucks, trains and anything to do with a ball.''

''What did he ask for at Christmas?''

Bryn's throat suddenly closed. This one she couldn't answer, not because she didn't remember but because the memory was too uncomfortable.

She'd never forget the way Ben had sat on the department store Santa's lap and asked for a daddy. Not a new car, or game, or even a puppy. But a daddy.

The Dillard department store Santa had looked at her

over the top of Ben's head and she felt like a failure. Worse yet, on Christmas morning Ben couldn't believe Santa Claus had forgotten the one thing he'd wanted— the one thing he'd asked for. Ben cried as though his heart were broken.

Ben's tears had nearly broken hers. It was then she decided to accept Stan's proposal.

"What did he want?" Kahlil persisted, unwilling to let the subject drop.

"A family," she answered softly, unable to meet his gaze.

"Why didn't you come to me?"

She shook her head, hot tears blinding her.

A minute passed before Kahlil spoke. "I don't know what makes me angrier. The fact you hid my child from me, or that you'd give him to another man."

The pain in his voice undid her, and she ached for the pain she'd unwittingly inflicted on the man she'd once loved beyond reason. She hadn't tried to give Ben away, but she could see how he'd think that.

Kahlil made a low, hoarse sound, part disgust, part despair. "You have no excuse, I see."

"None that you'd accept."

He slowly turned to look at her, his black hair hanging loose. "A real family would have been you and me, Bryn. Us together. That was the family he needed, that was the family we should have been."

Fresh tears flooded her eyes. She'd wanted a real family, too. It was the one thing she'd never had, not after her parents died, and it was her dearest wish for Ben, her greatest desire when she'd married Kahlil. But it hadn't worked out that way. Not for any of them.

Kahlil's hands clenched, muscles cording in his forearms. "I praise Allah that finally I have my son. I will make things right for him, but you...you...you're another matter entirely."

Just before takeoff he'd gone into the luxurious bedroom on the airplane and changed, removing the white linen shirt, putting on a black turtleneck and black blazer. Now, dressed in black from head to toe, he looked dark and powerful, a vengeful knight.

"Afraid, wife?" he murmured, his voice deep, threaded with warmth, curiosity, sensual huskiness.

He knew that even now, cornered, she responded to his strength, her senses alive, her emotions stirred. Heat crept to her cheeks and she ducked her head, throat working, heart racing.

And Kahlil, she knew, watched it all.

A man who had mastered sociology, anthropology, psychology before taking advance degrees in business and law, Kahlil had perfected people-watching to an art. It served him well, his powers of observation, he knew what people were feeling often before they recognized it themselves.

He knew her desire, her fear, her guilt. He knew he'd ripped her from her world and dragged her back into his. Going back to Zwar was like a time-travel into the dark ages. It was still feudal even barbaric, in its customs, particularly with regards to women. Yet Zwar was also a sensual place. A place of warmth and passion. Magic and mystery. It was the one place that felt like home. And it had been home. Until she let her insecurities pile up, until she placed her trust in the absolute wrong man.

Amin.

If only she'd gone to Kahlil with her worries, if only she'd been more patient, less…needy…

Trusting Amin had been like putting one's head in the mouth of a lion. Stupid, stupid immature decision. The lion bit. That's what lions do.

Kahlil watched the emotions flit across her face. Hope, anger, fear, despair. He had her worried now. Good. She should be worried. She should be very worried.

What was she thinking keeping his son from him? What kind of death wish did she have?

He'd fallen in love with her beauty, her laughter, her intelligence, but now he wondered if it had all been an illusion. Had his head been turned by her prettiness? Was she fair and golden without any substance beneath?

A shiny gold necklace…a gold gilding over cheap brass.

He swallowed hard, hands knotting, temper so hot he fought to keep it in check. He felt like a boiling cauldron, anger roiling, anger threatening to burn and destroy.

His gaze fell on her fair head bowed over the boy's. She held the child close to her breast, the child's cheek against her heart, his small lips parted in the bliss of sleep.

Oh, to be a child again, loved and protected, cradled against the harsh reality of life. Pain flickered briefly within, the flash of memory, another flash, this time of beautiful dark eyes, long dark hair, tears in his mother's eyes and a piercing cry as he was pulled from his mother's arms. *Mama! I want my Mama!*

He hated the memory and shoved it away, erasing all traces of a past that no longer mattered.

He'd lost his mother and survived. Ben would survive, too, if that's what fate decreed.

Yet seeing them together like this, Bryn and the boy, seeing the child's love and trust, and his wife's devotion made his chest tighten. If he came between them, it would destroy both Bryn and the boy. He'd shatter his own family, the very thing he'd vowed he'd never do.

But he wasn't the man that married Bryn. He wasn't a man who loved anymore. He wanted revenge. He wanted to punish. He wanted to break his wayward wife's spirit.

It didn't have to be like this. But she'd made her choice. Now he made his.

"Was there another man in Zwar?" he asked abruptly, turning from her, unable to look at the Madonna and child image another moment.

She would pay. Oh, how he'd make her pay.

"No." Her whispered voice reached his ears, a catch in her voice, tension in the answer.

She didn't answer with confidence. He heard the waver and the hint of guilt. Slowly he pivoted, took a step toward her. "You don't sound very sure of yourself. Would you like to think about the question a little longer?"

"I don't need to think about the question. I was faithful to you."

"Sexually?"

"Yes." Her voice hardened but red color rushed to her cheeks, heightening the blueness of her eyes, the paleness of her brow and chin. She looked like a painting, a Rueben, with the glow of red against her alabaster skin and the deep sapphire brilliance in her eyes.

"You're sure?"

"Quite sure."

"And emotionally?"

"My God, Kahlil, what kind of questions are these? If you suspect me of adultery then say so, but I won't play word games or guessing games with you. I've given you my answer and it's an honest answer. I never slept with another man while married to you. I never wanted to be with another man while married to you." The red wave of color began to recede, her cheeks turning a softer, paler pink, her lips quivering with emotion. "I just wanted you."

So why did she leave? His cold, analytical mind wanted to lacerate her tremulous words, cut through the softness to the truth. She was lying. Or she was hiding something. Either way, she'd deceived him and come precariously close to breaking his heart.

Thank God he'd recovered in time. Rifaat, his valet and personal assistant, had seen to that. Reminded Kahlil of his duties, his obligations, the future. The loss of his father helped focus him. Zwar mourned its leader and

Kahlil put his personal crisis behind him to focus on his country.

His work helped. For a time. Until he'd learned that Bryn was planning to marry again, and all the old emotions returned. The betrayal back, the pain resurfacing, the tangled emotions…anger, shock, disbelief. *I loved you. How could you walk away from me?*

It was the angry cry of a child forgotten. And he'd felt abandoned.

Kahlil despised the weakness within him, the need to love and be loved. He shouldn't feel such a need for people, or relationships. His father had never married again after his mother was gone. Why couldn't he be as strong?

"What am I doing with you here?" he gritted. "What am I thinking?"

She sat forward, expression brightening. "You can turn the plane around. It's not too late. We haven't even crossed the Atlantic yet."

Her eagerness to escape infuriated him all over again. Who was she to make decisions? She ran away. She left him. She may have even cheated on him.

"If I send you back, I send you alone."

She looked confused, forehead furrowing and then suddenly she understood. "And Ben?"

Kahlil felt cold, hard, strong. "He is the crown prince. One day he will inherit my title, and position as leader of my people. He, of course, remains with me."

She stirred, panic in her eyes, panic in her sudden restless motions. "I'll go to the ambassador—"

"And what do you hope the ambassador will do? The child is mine. As his father, I have rights. Not even the American government will argue that point."

"They won't allow you to keep him from me!"

"Of course not. And I have no intention of keeping you and the boy apart. You are free to come and go, visiting as often as you like, but Ben will remain at the palace in Tiva."

"Without me?"

"He's young. He'd adjust." He heard the harshness in his voice and he didn't care. She'd deprived him of the first three years of his child's life. She deserved whatever she got.

"You'd break his heart."

"Hearts mend. Wounds heal. I know."

"And knowing what you know, you'd still hurt him like that?"

"You are in no position to lecture me. You were never going to let me be part of his life. You were determined to keep him to yourself." His upper lip curled, a primal snarl he couldn't conceal. "In a few years Zwar will be his home, and my people his people. Ben will love the adventure of it, and he'll be blessed with wealth, position and opportunity."

"You can't buy him, or his affections!"

He shrugged, glad to see her squirm. He'd shaken her.

"I want to call the ambassador," she demanded. "Now."

"I'm sorry. The phone isn't working."

"That's not true. You made some calls earlier."

"But that was earlier. This is now."

"Kahlil, you have no right—"

"I have every right!"

His voice thundered, waking Ben. Bryn tried to hush her son back to sleep but Ben was definitely awake, lifting his head and sleepily gazing around the cabin.

"Are we there yet?" he asked with a yawn, brown eyes blinking, a worried crease between his jet-black eyebrows.

"No, not yet," she soothed, pressing a kiss to his forehead, silently cursing Kahlil for waking Ben, and waking him in the middle of a fight. This is exactly what she wanted to protect Ben from. But Ben wasn't about to go back to sleep, not when he sensed so much tension in the air.

Tipping his head back, he stared into her face, one small hand reaching out to touch her mouth. "Why are you yelling?"

It was on the tip of her tongue to reply that it was Kahlil yelling, Kahlil being impossible, but she couldn't say that, none of it. Whatever her feelings were for Kahlil, she couldn't allow them to influence Ben. He'd need to establish his own relationship with Kahlil, without prejudices from her.

"Was I yelling?" she murmured, struggling to modulate her voice, and calm her racing pulse. This was a long trip, a long night, she had to get her emotions under control.

"Yes. You were yelling at that man."

That man. Your father.

She looked up, pained, her gaze settling on Kahlil. In his black turtleneck and his blazer, Kahlil looked darkly forbidding, his beautiful features hard, his expression contemptuous.

''I'm sorry,'' she answered. ''I shouldn't yell. It hurts peoples ears, doesn't it?''

''Yes,'' Ben agreed, sitting up and wrapping his small, cool fingers around hers. ''Who is that man? Why is he with us?''

Pain tugged at her heart. She couldn't lie, couldn't ignore the question, either. Ben needed to know the truth, and he'd find out soon, if not now, then quickly after they landed. Far better to hear it from her.

''Ben, this is…your…'' Her gaze lifted, her eyes meeting Kahlil's. She found no warmth in his expression, no compassion in his golden eyes. Bryn dropped her gaze, focusing on Ben, trying to blot out the image of a seething Kahlil. ''Ben, this man, he's your…is your…''

''Daddy.''

Kahlil said it, completed the sentence, his voice crackling with anger.

It wasn't the way she wanted it said. Not with so much anger and force. Not with that kind of arrogance, either.

''Yes,'' she hurriedly agreed, hoping to soften things, ease the tension. ''He is your daddy. We were married a long time ago and lived in a beautiful desert.''

''A beautiful desert?'' Ben looked past Bryn to Kahlil. ''In a tent? With camels?''

"In a palace," Kahlil replied. "But we do have camels."

Ben sat up even straighter, using his palm to push away from her chest. "I like camels." He looked so serious, his expression exactly like Kahlil's. "I am Ben," he said firmly, precisely, dark eyes frowning, black eyebrows furrowed in concentration. "That's my name. What is yours?"

"Sheikh Kahlil Hasim al-Assad."

"That's a lot of names."

"Not so many. Soon you will have a name like mine, too."

"Okay."

Okay. That was all it took. Ben accepted it, accepted the new father, the new name, the new home just like that.

Ben looked at her, touched her cheek with his fingertips. "This is my real daddy?" he whispered, with a swift glance at Kahlil.

"Yes."

"The one I wanted?"

"The one you wanted, my baby."

No one spoke. Bryn's pulse raced. She could sense Ben's struggle, his confusion and questions. Everything had changed for him just like that. Suddenly Ben thrust a hand out to Kahlil. "I'm Ben, Daddy."

Kahlil's features hardened, his jaw granite-tight. For a moment he didn't move, his expression closed and grim. And then slowly, very slowly he reached out with his own hand and took his son's. "I'm pleased to meet you, Ben. It's good we're finally together."

Ben nodded solemnly. "It's been a long time."

Kahlil's dark gaze lifted, his eyes met Bryn's and held. "A very long time."

# CHAPTER FIVE

THE Learjet made its final approach and landed soundlessly on the asphalt runway. Minutes later it came to a smooth stop in front of a low, brightly lit building.

Before the jet's door opened, a grim Kahlil emerged from the private bedroom cabin, his Western clothes hidden by his robe, the *djellaba,* and a white *howli* concealing his dark hair. Bryn's stomach did somersaults and she swallowed hard, lumps swelling her throat closed.

Sheikh Kahlil al-Assad. In person.

He turned, glanced her direction, his flinty gaze inspecting her hair and dress. "You must cover yourself."

"It might seem strange to Ben," she replied, placing an uneasy hand on the top of her son's head.

His gaze met hers and held. After a tense silence, he answered. "It will seem more strange to him if you force me to take action."

Kahlil didn't understand. Ben might be half Arab, but he'd never been exposed to Middle Eastern customs. He didn't know anything of the language or the culture. "Just give me a chance to explain to him first."

Kahlil's mouth compressed, contemptuously. "I think I should be the one to explain. After all, wearing the *djellaba* and *howli* are *my* customs. I understand far better than you.''

And he did explain, in a matter of thirty seconds, saying without apology that the robe and veil made women special, protecting pretty women and turning them into princesses. ''Would you like your mom to be a princess?''

Ben smiled, a small shy smile, and hesitantly nodded. ''Put it on, Mommy. I want to see you be a princess.''

Kahlil had trapped her. Again. She stood immobile while Kahlil unfolded a long black *djellaba* and another shorter cloth. His hands moved quickly, settling the robe across her shoulders and then the veil over her head. She felt the brush of his fingers at her temple and then against her mouth.

Fresh tears filled her eyes. She wanted him, but not like this. She wanted him when they loved only each other, believed only in the other.

Suddenly he leaned forward and pressed a kiss to her mouth, through the thin fabric of the veil. ''We're home,'' he said quietly, victorious. ''Remember where you are now. Remember who you are now.''

She couldn't speak, the air bottled in her chest and the fine hairs tingled at her nape. Fear, fatigue and anxiety overwhelmed her. She felt unbalanced, torn between her own need and Ben's needs realizing that they weren't the same and wouldn't ever be the same again.

Ben tugged at the black robe and she stepped back to see him. He wrinkled his nose as he inspected her clothes. ''She doesn't look like a princess,'' he said, disappointed, even a little disgusted. "Princesses don't wear dresses like that."

She'd read him too many stories, told him too many fantastic versions of Cinderella, Snow White, Sleeping Beauty. He knew princesses were soft, sweet magical creatures, nothing like the dark robed mother in front of him.

Bryn would have smiled if the situation weren't so serious. She curled an arm around his waist, and hugged him to her legs. "It's okay," she answered quickly. "The robe is to help Mommy. It's a costume, something fun and new."

"But he said, the daddy said, you'd be a princess. I want you to look like a princess. Take it off," he insisted, tugging harder on the robe, trying to draw it away from her legs. "Please, Mommy, take it off now."

"She can't," Kahlil said quietly but firmly, crouching next to Ben. "And your mommy understands. She's not upset. She knows why she needs to wear it."

"Why?" Tears shone in Ben's eyes, his lower lip thrust, curling with weariness and petulance.

"Because we're in my country, and it's a different country with different rules. We treat our women very special and we like to protect them. If your mommy wears this robe, she'll be safe."

"It's magic? Like a spell?" Kahlil had caught Ben's imagination again, and the tears dried in his eyes.

"A little like that. And she won't wear it forever, just until we reach the palace."

"But it's not a nice color. It should be a pretty color.

Like pink, or blue. Mommy looks pretty in pink or blue.''

"Then let's pick her out a pretty dress when we reach the palace. We'll look at all the beautiful dresses and you tell me which ones would be nice on your beautiful mommy.'' Kahlil stood, extended a hand. "Now, let's go see the palace.''

They were moving across the tarmac into the brightly lit building when sudden shouts drew a virtual army of soldiers from the building and the airport perimeter.

"What's happening?'' Bryn cried, turning to Kahlil.

He shook his head. "I don't know,'' he replied, swinging Benjamin into his arms.

Bryn wanted Ben, needed him with her but the soldiers were converging, carrying enormous guns that filled her with terror.

One soldier approached Kahlil, bowed deeply and murmured something in Arabic.

Kahlil nodded curtly, picked up his pace and drew Ben even closer to his chest. He cast a brief glance in Bryn's direction but his expression revealed nothing.

They were practically running. She noted that the soldiers had formed a tight protective circle around Kahlil and herself and that a spotlight was sweeping the tarmac, casting a great white blinding light behind them.

Inside the building the door slammed shut and the soldiers moved, separating Bryn from Kahlil.

"Ben!'' she cried, reaching out for him, but the soldiers stepped toward her, distancing her further from Kahlil and her child.

Her mouth tasted like sawdust and she swallowed convulsively, realizing it was fear making her throat seal close. What was happening? Where were they taking her? Where were Kahlil and Ben going?

She hadn't realized she'd voiced the questions aloud until a crisp voice answered her in nearly flawless English, "No harm will come to you. Please be patient, Princess. All questions will be answered in due time."

Be patient? How? Ben was gone and soldiers were relentless, never once touching her, but moving her continually forward, leading her through an unmarked door and out into the night.

A car awaited, a black luxury-style car, a Mercedes she guessed, and the back door opened. She had no choice but to climb in and the door slammed shut, the car swiftly pulling away.

"Where are we going?" she asked the driver, hands balling in her lap.

The driver briefly glanced into the rearview mirror, dark eyes flashing, but he didn't speak, and just as swiftly his attention returned to the road.

She'd asked the question not really expecting an answer. In Zwar, men did not address strange women, especially Western women, but she'd felt compelled to assert herself, to try to make sense of the chaos at the airport.

"What happened back there?" she persisted. "Why so many soldiers?"

The driver didn't even glance into the rearview mirror this time. He simply continued driving.

Bryn leaned against the seat, fear and indignation wrestling for the upper hand. How could Kahlil do this to her? And yet thank God he had Ben. No one would touch Ben if Kahlil held him. And Kahlil would protect him, she knew that much. He might hate her, but he already loved his son.

Massive gates opened to accept the limousine, only to shut loudly after the car passed through the compound's high stone walls. Bryn felt relieved when they finally reached the palace. She wanted only to see Ben again. To know that he was safe.

Inside the palace, the guards silently handed her off to two robed servants, one which she recognized immediately as Rifaat, Kahlil's personal assistant. Part butler, part secretary, Rifaat al Surakh handled Kahlil's private affairs, business as well as personal. In the past he'd managed everything from travel arrangements to political gatherings.

Bryn felt a momentary glow, relieved to see her old friend again. "Rifaat, how are you?"

"Well, thank you, Princess," he returned, bowing deeply. The son of a diplomat, he'd been educated in the West, attending prestigious Georgetown University in Washington D.C., before returning to Zwar and serving in the diplomatic corps like his father before him.

Bright, sophisticated, modern, Rifaat had always been her friend. "Rifaat, help me, please. The soldiers at the airport, they took my baby from me. Is he here? What happened?''

Rifaat bowed again. ''I shall escort you to your rooms, Princess.''

''No, I don't want to go to my room. I must see Kahlil. He has my son. Are they here? Have they arrived?''

The second manservant silently walked away, leaving Rifaat and Bryn alone. With the second man gone, Rifaat bowed a third time. ''I am to escort you to the ladies' quarters. Your maid is waiting for you there.''

I must see Kahlil,'' she repeated firmly, squaring her shoulders. ''Please, Rifaat. My *son.*''

His eyes flashed, his gaze briefly meeting hers, before he looked away, staring at a point just past her shoulder. He didn't look at her again. He didn't intend to speak.

''Rifaat, *please.*''

''Your room has been prepared,'' he repeated woodenly, carefully keeping his gaze fixed on the marble pillar behind her. ''I hope you find it satisfactory.''

She blanched, as if he'd thrown a glass of icy cold water in her face. He didn't intend to tell her anything. Even if he knew where Kahlil was, Rifaat wouldn't share his information with her. They might have been friends five years ago but they weren't friends now.

Turning, Rifaat set off down the marble hall, his slippered feet noiseless on the gleaming black-and-white marble floor. She followed behind him, having no other choice. No one would deal with her here, not until Kahlil had given instructions.

At the elaborately carved entry to the east wing, the wing where the women lived, a veiled maid appeared and bowed to Bryn. Kahlil's valet walked away without a look back.

He'd done his duty, she thought bitterly. He'd escorted her to the harem. He could get her off his hands.

She stared after him, watching the valet's departing back. He treated her the way Kahlil had treated her—with anger, with scorn, with contempt.

She flushed faintly, the skin hot and tight across her cheekbones. Only one thing could be worse than her current situation. The return of Amin.

The young maid introduced herself as Lalia and announced that she would be the princess' personal assistant, helping with dressing and hair and happiness.

Bryn nearly smiled at the peculiar description of services to be rendered. Dressing and hair and happiness. As if life were so easy.

But Bryn didn't smile and Lalia shot a shy, nervous smile at her as she led Bryn into her private suite of rooms. "For you, my lady," Lalia said, gesturing around the spacious high-ceiling bedroom. Her English was stilted, her accent heavy. "You like, my lady?"

"Lalia," Bryn spoke gently, persuasively. "My husband, the sheikh, I must see him. He has my son, and I'm afraid."

"No fears," Lalia replied, rustling her hands like flower petals in a breeze. "Everything is lovely here. Just the way you like, yes?"

"My son—"

"This room, very pretty, yes?"

Lalia wouldn't tell her anything, either. The girl wouldn't even acknowledge Bryn's pain.

No one would.

Slowly, numbly, Bryn wandered to the middle of the room, her old room, the same one she'd had three and a half years ago, and glanced at the pale peach carpet beneath her feet.

The carpet's pattern was intricate, vines and scrolls and ornate vases, a priceless wool carpet made seven hundred years ago for a Persian queen, reputedly the most beautiful woman in the East. Kahlil had bought the carpet for her, installed it in her room. He wanted everything perfect for his bride, his future queen.

It hadn't worked out that way.

Her gaze fell on the small, elegant carved wood chest sitting next to her bed on the night table.

Her jewelry box.

Amin. The struggle. Her last night at the palace three and a half years ago.

Her heart did a ragged double-beat, revulsion radiating from her middle to her arms and legs, making her shake. She took an involuntary step backward as if she could put space between her and memories of the past.

Slowly she crossed to the nightstand and even more slowly lifted the dark heavy lid on the box. Diamonds, sapphires, rubies, emeralds sparkled in a sea of purple velvet.

Couldn't be. She'd taken it all, emptying the box into

her purse before fleeing the palace, dumping the glittering jewelry—bangles, chokers, drop earrings, a gold-and-diamond crusted tiara—all presents from Kahlil, into her handbag. She'd used the jewelry to buy her way out of Zwar, smuggling herself onto a charter flight to New York and then another flight, this one on a commercial liner to Dallas where Rose had picked her up from the airport.

But the jewels were all here, or perhaps they were merely replacements, a tiara for a tiara, gold bangles for gold bangles. Her chest tightened with sorrow and fresh pain.

He believed Amin but not her. He'd trusted Amin but not her.

Bryn lowered the jewelry box lid, the lid closing with a hollow little thud, much like her heart in her chest.

She sat down slowly on the edge of the bed, her hands braced on either side of her hips, her fingers outstretched on the smooth silk coverlet. She was stricken at the memory of her last night in the palace, in this room. Amin had trapped her here, his mouth had covered hers to stifle her scream. He'd tasted sour, of alcohol and old cigarettes, and he'd used his weight to pin her on the bed.

''My lady, this is your old room, yes? You like room, yes?''

Old room… Yes. Bryn shivered, blinked and forced herself to pull out of the past and focus on Lalia. It was her old room. A room that had given her nightmares for years.

Bryn stood up, crossed her arms over her chest. She felt disgust and fury that she was being trapped in this room—in this life—again. "I'm sorry, but I can't stay here. You'll have to tell his highness this room won't do."

Lalia opened her mouth but before she could speak, Bryn marched to the door. "Never mind, I'll tell him myself."

Bryn got nowhere. Guards outside the women's quarters wouldn't let her pass. They simply stood there, two abreast, and shook their heads. "Don't make me scream."

The guards didn't even blink.

So she screamed, loudly, shockingly loudly, screaming as though she were being hurt, even murdered, and no one came.

And the soldiers didn't move.

Only Lalia fell to Bryn's feet weeping. "Please, Princess, please, Princess, please."

"Lalia, stop!"

"Princess, you'll get me in trouble. I shall be very punished for displeasing you."

The girl was clutching Bryn's feet, pressing her lips to Bryn's ankle bones. "Lalia!"

But the girl continued to beg, muttering teary incoherent things in Arabic, speaking so rapidly that Bryn only picked up words and brief phrases. "Lalia, no one will punish you."

"His lord highness will!"

"That's not true."

Lalia cast a fearful glance at the guards. "My lady," she choked, pressing her wet face against Bryn's shin, "your last girl was sent to very bad place. Please, Princess, do not have send me away, too."

Bryn felt a rush of remorse. Was that true? Had Adjia, her first maid, been punished? "I must see his highness. I must," she said more quietly.

"And you will. His highness will call for you. I know. I am sure. Now come, Princess, have some tea."

Kahlil had been home only three hours and already he'd received a phone call from Amin.

He slowly hung up the receiver and stared at the photograph on his office desk, a silver-framed photo Amin had given him of the two of them. The picture had been snapped after a polo match a number of years ago. Amin had his arm slung around Kahlil's neck and they were laughing at a joke Amin had made. They looked like the best of friends.

For a while Kahlil had thought they were best friends, or at least very good friends.

But that changed a long, long time ago—back before they were adults with duties. Responsibilities. Kahlil wondered when friendship had turned to envy. When genuine affection had transformed into manipulation.

During their twenties they had still laughed, continued to share a joke and spend an evening together, but it wasn't without tension. And guilt. Kahlil didn't need to be reminded that fate had treated them differently— Kahlil the crown prince. Amin, the poor relation.

And now Amin wanted to come home again, to return to Zwar for a visit. Amin had only been back once in three and a half years, and that was for an afternoon, for Kahlil's father's funeral. They hadn't even talked then. Amin acted as if the funeral was merely a government formality.

So why did Amin want to return to Tiva now? Why not six months ago? Six weeks ago? Six months from now?

It couldn't be because of Bryn, could it?

Kahlil picked up the framed photograph. He studied Amin's boyishly handsome face, the light gray eyes, the laughing mouth.

Maybe it was time he put to rest the rumors, and the speculation. If there was something between Bryn and Amin he might as well find out now.

Kahlil returned the photo to his desk and reached for the phone again. Swiftly he punched the numbers to Amin's apartment in Monte Carlo. Amin answered almost right away.

"I've thought it over," Kahlil said coolly. "You're right. It has been a long time since we've been together. Come home. Let's catch up."

Bryn watched the maid unpack the small overnight bag that managed to make the trip from Dallas.

Silently, industriously, Lalia tucked Bryn's handful of lingerie and undergarments into the clothing wardrobe. But her expression changed when she pulled the dresses and pantsuit from the bottom of the bag. "These are not for Princess," she said.

But I don't want to be a princess, Bryn thought in exasperation from her perch on the foot of the bed. She just wanted to be Bryn, a twenty-four-year-old mother with a small but sincere circle of friends. She'd made a good life for herself in Texas; it might not have been fancy, and she might have lived off limited means, but it was her life and she wasn't complaining.

Lalia hung up Bryn's dresses but did so with obvious distaste. She opened up the second wardrobe door and gestured to the rainbow of color inside. Turquoise, royal-blue, violet, rose, peach, lemon-yellow, ivory, white, gold. Silks, chiffon, satin, velvets. Long gowns beaded and embroidered, jewel encrusted. "For Princess," Lalia said, "You like?"

Incredible. How long had those dresses been hanging in the closet? How much had Kahlil invested in them while waiting for her to return?

Her jewelry box was full. The wardrobe an abundance of delicate fabrics and vibrant color. Gold slippers lined on the floor.

It was how it had been before. It was how Kahlil determined it would be again. Everything had changed but nothing was different.

Incredible. Excruciating. Bryn felt a torment of guilt, realizing how hard it must have been for Kahlil to wait for her, understanding for the first time that he had never intended their marriage to end. He'd merely given her time.

He'd wanted her back.

Lalia gently closed the wardrobe doors and turned to face Bryn. "Everything is ready. Come, we shall draw your bath."

Undressing in the marble bathroom, Bryn caught a glimpse of herself in the massive gilt-framed mirror. Her long hair hung lank, blue shadows dimmed the brightness of her eyes. She felt like hell and she looked it, too.

"My lady, the bath is hot, yes, see? Please, sit." Lalia gestured to the gold sunken tub set in white marble shot with streaks of gray. The tub's faucets were gold. The sink and fixtures were gold. Marble and gold. Real gold. Solid gold. A bathroom fit for a queen.

Fragrant steam rose from the gold tub, flower petals floated on the water's surface.

Bryn dropped her towel, shy but resigned to the palace's lack of privacy. The palace maids were too well trained, too fearful of displeasing to not fulfill their duties, and their duties were many. It was their job to serve, to assist, to make the princess's life comfortable.

Suddenly Kahlil's voice grated, shattering the quiet. "Leave us," he said, voice echoing in the polished marble bath. "I wish to speak to my wife. *Alone.*"

Lalia fled the room, bowing, scraping, whimpering worshiping words that drove Bryn crazy.

Bryn's first impulse was to leap from the tub and grab a towel, but she found herself frozen, reclining beneath the rose strewn scented water in shock. "What are you doing here? Where's Ben?"

"Which question should I answer first?"

She felt her blood begin to boil. "Ben, please. Where is he? And what on earth happened at the airport?"

"It doesn't concern you."

"There isn't any real threat, is there? I won't have Ben subjected to unrest or instability."

"Your imagination runs away with you again. It was a protective measure, nothing more than that."

"I don't like being separated from Ben and I want him back."

He turned his face to the door. "Unfortunately you're not getting him back."

"Kahlil!"

"Sorry, but it's the truth. I'm removing him from your care until I know what to do."

"About what?" she demanded, her temper growing hotter.

"As a crown prince, the boy will need a very special education. He will require challenging coursework, intensive study of languages and exposure to European and Eastern cultures."

"He's three. Practically a baby!"

"I was sent to England not much older than Ben is now. It's better if we begin preparing him for his duty soon—"

"*No!*" The protest was wrung from her, her voice strangled. "I will never send him away. I will not have strangers raise my son."

Slowly he pivoted to face her, his gold gaze narrowing, black lashes lowering as he studied her reclining figure. Her knees, her pale bare thighs, her tummy, the rise of her breasts. "The matter's out of your hands. We're in Zwar. Your opinion holds no weight."

She sat upright, anger jackknifing in her middle. "If you think I'll bow and scrape like Lalia then you've another think coming, Sheikh al-Assad. I might be back in Tiva, but I'm not the clinging, fragile girl you married all those years ago. I'm stronger, and this time I have a voice."

In the hours since she and Kahlil had been parted at the airport, her husband had showered and changed, leaving Western clothes behind to dress in a traditional robe. He looked distant, detached. "If you had a voice, wouldn't I hear it?"

Confusion made her stop and think. "Yes…"

"Then why didn't I hear it earlier when you screamed?"

He'd heard her this afternoon, heard her cry and ignored it. Brilliant pain, hot and blinding, shot through her. Cupping a handful of water, she threw it at him, and again, liberally splashing him.

Kahlil leaned over and hauled her out of the bath onto the cool, slick marble floor. "You've done it now."

Goose pimples covered her flesh. "Be mad at me, but don't take Ben away. I don't know what kind of game you're playing, but it's not fair, and it's not right."

He dragged her against him, hip to hip, thigh to thigh,

their bodies pressed lightly. "This isn't a game. The games are over. The consequences begin."

Hot, cold, she felt feverish and sick. "Punishing Ben isn't fair."

"I'm not punishing Ben, I'm punishing you. You lied to me, deceived me, stole from me—"

Fear filled her limbs like cold wet cement. "If you're talking about the jewelry—"

"I'm talking about my son. He is mine, isn't he?"

"Of course he's yours. Just look at him! *Your* eyes, *your* nose, *your* mouth. He's you all over."

"Then my actions are justified."

Closing the last bit of distance between them, he pressed her naked, shivering body more tightly to him and covered her mouth with his. It was a soul-searching kiss, drawing her breath from her lungs, drinking her protests into him.

He kissed her until her legs buckled and tiny yellow spots danced against the darkness of her mind. She was trembling, clutching his robe, feeling the rapid thud of his heart through his chest.

"I am sorry," he murmured, lifting his head, his golden eyes filled with a silent pain he couldn't, wouldn't articulate. "I have to do this for my country, and my people. There is no other way."

His body was warm, the hard planes of muscle curving tautly beneath the press of her palms. She felt him against her, felt his heat and strength and remembered what it had been like to lie with him, and love him, and be loved by him. "If you try to take him from me," she choked, "I will fight you for him, every second of every hour of every day."

"And you will lose."

"I have no choice but to fight. He is my hope."

"Mine, too."

## CHAPTER SIX

BRYN couldn't stop pacing her bedroom floor, replaying the scene in the bathroom over and over in her mind, trying to forget the feel of his lips against hers, the strength of his body. He'd kissed her to punish her and yet his mouth had been anything but hard, his touch anything but unkind. She felt the old desire flicker there and burst into flame. He still wanted her but this time he wanted her for revenge.

She shivered, appalled by her response to him, and the fact that she could be attracted to a man who could wrest her son away from her. But Kahlil wasn't just any man. He was her husband. Ben's father.

Ben's father.

Oh God, what had she done? How could she have thought she'd get away with keeping Ben's parentage a secret? Kahlil was one of the wealthiest, most powerful men in the world. He was bound to find out. If not now, then later, when Ben was older and pressing to know more about his birth father. Children wanted to know these things. They had a right to know these things.

Bryn felt fresh guilt and concern. She knew instinctively that Kahlil would never hurt Ben...at least never consciously. But could he do so unconsciously? Unwittingly?

Arguing with Kahlil had always been difficult. He was intelligent, quick, eloquent. He mashed her words. Turned her arguments around so that in the end she was just contradicting herself, flustered and tongue-tied.

But now, Kahlil wouldn't even argue. He stated his opinions as facts and expected her to submit. But this wasn't the Middle Ages and she wasn't a woman raised in a harem.

She understood Kahlil's anger and frustration. She realized he needed time to sort his emotions out. But she wasn't about to allow Kahlil to strip her out of her rights.

Ben was her son. He was only three and even though he was a bright, adventurous little boy, he was also quite sensitive. He must be wondering where she was. He must be anxious to see her.

If Kahlil wouldn't bring Ben to her, then she would go to him.

The palace was dark. Serenely still. Bryn felt a thrill ripple down her spine as she tiptoed past Lalia's cot in the outer room and into the shadowy hall.

Moonlight dappled the marble floor and Bryn crept from the women's quarters to the main reception rooms and down another wing to the guest quarters. She was sure Kahlil had sent Ben there. There weren't many options. The men's quarter, the women's, the guest rooms, and then the sheikh's private suite.

She slowly opened the first door and peered into the room which was lit only by moonlight. The window was unshuttered and the large, low bed was empty.

Carefully she closed the door, moved to the next and repeated the inspection. Empty room. Empty bed.

At the third door she felt a tremor. Her senses were taut, her anxiety high. It was more frightening creeping around the palace than she'd anticipated and for a moment she had the unnerving sensation of being followed.

Ridiculous. Everybody was asleep. No one stirred.

Bryn pushed the door wider. The room looked inky and full of shadows. With the curtains drawn she could just make out a shape. She caught a sudden movement from the corner of her eye and her instincts screamed for her to run.

Lights flooded the spacious bedchamber, unusually bright lights blinding her. Hands clamped on her forearms, lifting her off her feet.

"Let me go!" Bryn swung out with her arms and legs, kicking, elbows flying. "Put me down!"

"Stop it, Bryn. You're only making this worse."

With a sinking sensation in the pit of her stomach, she heard the rasp of Kahlil's voice and caught a glimpse of his profile. His jaw was shadowed with the beginnings of a beard. "How…what…?"

"Motion detectors," he said shortly, making sense of her incoherence, even as he dragged her past a bevy of palace guards clustered in the doorway. Another cluster of guards stood at the far end of the marble hallway watching. "State-of-the-art security. The moment you left your room my surveillance camera turned on."

Mortification flooded her veins with fresh adrenaline. He'd *watched* her tiptoe through the palace. He'd watched her search through the rooms. "You're a Peeping Tom!"

"And you're a sneak," he retorted grimly, his white robe parted revealing far more skin than Bryn was comfortable with.

He looked raw and primitive and incredibly male— which is exactly what had gotten her into trouble five years ago. "I wouldn't have to sneak around if you'd just let me see my son!"

"I have never met such a disobedient woman in my life."

"I'm sorry you've been so sheltered, but I have to tell you there are hundreds—thousands—of women who are certain to be more difficult than me." Bryn yanked on her arm, struggling to free herself. "Now let me go!"

"Not an option." He swung her into his arms and clasped her firmly against his chest. "I cannot sleep with you wandering the palace, and my guards will get no rest if I return you to your room. You'll stay with me tonight. And I promise you, you'll go nowhere."

Kahlil kicked the door shut behind him. The tall tapered candles in the wall sconces flickered, casting dancing shadows on the smooth plaster walls and center columns. She shivered, feeling as though he'd carried her back in time. "Candles?"

"More restful." He dropped her on his bed, the midnight-blue velvet coverlet creasing, the dark velvet gleaming like water beneath the moon.

It crossed her mind that she was truly in trouble now.

Kahlil would never hurt her—she trusted him with her life—but being alone with him like this was incredibly dangerous. She'd never been able to resist his warmth, nor his strength.

Bryn swallowed and grabbed handfuls of the velvet coverlet, crushing the soft fabric against her skin. "What do you intend to do?"

"Lock you up."

Her heart did a painful leap, like a skydiver jumping off a cliff. "I'm serious."

"So am I." He shot her a peculiar glance as he drew a dark carved wood box from his ornate wardrobe. "Runaway wives ruin reputations."

She cast a wary look at the wood box and then up into his face. His expression was blank, frighteningly so. "You don't need to worry about my reputation. I'm fine. I'll be fine."

"It's my reputation that concerns me." He closed the wardrobe doors and turned toward her. The box in the crook of his arm was heavy enough to tense his forearm, muscles drawn, delineated, every part of him beautifully made.

"Just what is that?"

He shifted the box from his arm to the bed. "Instruments of my pleasure."

"Very funny." She stared uneasily at the lid of the box, the dark wood carved into fanciful designs; serpents encircling a tree, doves against a vine, the limbs of a man and woman intimately entwined. Not an innocent box. Not an innocent man.

''You think I'm joking?'' His black hair gleaming in the candlelight.

Maybe not. He was seriously humor-impaired, but before she could say a thing, even as she touched the tip of her tongue to her rapidly drying upper lip, he snapped the lid open, revealing the contents.

Bright gold gleamed against scarlet silk.

Bryn blinked. Thick gold bands nestled against blood-red silk. Her heart did a second, but equally painful jump. What were those? What was Kahlil planning to do?

As he leaned forward, lifting the gold bangles from the box, his robe shifted, revealing more of the hard planes of his chest, the muscles taut beneath the gleam of skin. She could just catch a whiff of the sandalwood fragrance he wore, exotic, spicy, erotic. Heat flooded her veins, her body craving his.

But the rush of desire died a quick death when Kahlil opened one of the gold bangles and snapped it shut around her slim wrist.

''You're handcuffing me?'' Her voice rose to a fevered pitch. Just who the hell did he think he was?

''I'll do what I have to do.''

''This in unacceptable, Kahlil, even from you.'' She tried to shake off the band but he'd secured it tightly, clasping it on one of the smallest locks. It pinched, too, not terribly, but just enough to remind her she was trapped.

Furious, she shook her arm again. The blasted handcuff weighed at least a pound. Had to be solid gold. No other reason for it to be so heavy.

"I had to curtail your wanderlust."

"I just wanted to see Ben."

Utterly remorseless, he opened the second gold band, this connected to the one on her wrist by a long, thick gold chain. "And I'd already told you no. What part of 'no' don't you understand?"

Tears started to her eyes, tears of shame and anger. "The part where you tell me to jump and I'm expected to do your bidding." She jerked on the chain, nearly pulling the second handcuff from his hold. "Do you enjoy degrading women?"

"Of course not, but I enjoy peace of mind, and you, woman, give me none." He snapped the second handcuff to his own wrist, linking them together.

She'd expected him to shackle her to the bed. It hadn't crossed her mind he'd lock her to him. She stared at the three-foot gold chain in alarm. Tethered. Trapped. His prisoner.

Could the punishment be worse? "I'm not going to spend the night locked up like a criminal!"

"You're lucky I haven't had you arrested. The thought has crossed my mind. Several times."

"I haven't broken any laws."

"Any? Try a half dozen. You'd be treated harshly in our court, too. We don't look kindly on rebellious women."

"So send me to prison. Explain that to Ben!"

"I wouldn't have to tell Ben you went to prison. I

could always say you chose to leave. You wanted to go home, and so you did.''

"Leaving him here, without me?"

Kahlil shrugged, tightened the second shackle, and tugged on the heavy gold chain. Bryn fell forward, at the mercy of Kahlil's whim. "Mothers are human. They make mistakes. Change their minds. Run from responsibility all the time.''

"Not me."

He shrugged again. "To tell you the truth, Bryn, I don't really care. I've been up over forty-eight hours without sleep, crossed the Atlantic twice, saved you from an imprudent wedding, discovered a son. I'm tired. I just want sleep.''

"I'd rather be thrown into a pit of vipers!"

An eyebrow lifted. "How melodramatic, even from you.''

She changed her approach, gentled her tone. She had to make him see reason. "Kahlil, you know I'm a light sleeper. How can I rest like this?''

"That's your problem, not mine. You should have thought about the consequences before you snuck out of the harem. However, what's done is done and now we'll go to bed.''

"I will not sleep with you."

"*Bryn,* you are trying my patience. Can't you see I am doing my best to take care of you?''

She tugged furiously on the chain linking them. "This is your idea of taking care of me? My God, you aren't fit to be a father!''

His expression suddenly darkened, brows lowering, his features hard and cold. She'd struck a nerve. Oh, how she'd struck a nerve!

"If you want to live to see the morning, I'd lie down, and be very, very quiet. I'm tired of you making a fool out of me. I need sleep. You need supervision. I'm sorry I'm forced to treat you like a farm animal, but this is the only solution I can think of."

"A farm animal! I'll show you a farm animal—" She broke off to give the chain a violent yank. His arm didn't even move. He didn't even wobble. She pulled harder, with every bit of her strength, fighting to knock him off balance but Kahlil didn't budge. He simply stood there, immobile, allowing himself the smallest smile of pleasure.

Damn his six-foot-three-inch body. Damn his immense shoulders and solid thighs. Damn the muscles and skin and his incredible warm, spicy scent. "I hate you!"

He smiled, all teeth. "The feeling is mutual, darling. So go to bed and save us both another scene." And with that, he tossed back the velvet comforter, revealing dark gold satin sheets and practically threw her into bed.

Then he stripped—stripped!—peeling his white cotton trousers off his lean hips and shrugging out of the white robe.

The gold chain linking them jingled as he slid into bed next to her, the mattress giving slightly, satin sheets cool and smooth against her heated skin.

"Do you have to sleep naked?" she gritted, trying to

block out the image of his large body stretched carelessly next to hers.

He rolled to his side, the chain between them momentarily tightening, the gold satin sheet sliding low on his waist, emphasizing his deep chest and wide shoulders. ''We're married. This is about as sexless as it gets.''

Blood rushed to her cheeks. ''What about the candles? Aren't you going to blow them out?''

''Not tonight. I'm going to need them to keep an eye on you. Besides, they'll burn out eventually. Close to morning.'' He reached out, touched a long silvery-blond strand of hair. ''And Bryn, you won't be able to break this chain. Don't try. It'll just be a waste of energy.''

She glanced at the gold chain stretched between them, still shocked he'd actually handcuff her to him. What kind of man handcuffs a woman? A medieval man. That's the kind of man, she answered herself darkly. And a man without the least bit of modesty. How could he climb into bed with her without a scrap of clothing on? For heaven's sake, the satin sheet revealed far more than it hid, outlining the hard, carved planes of his body.

''If this is the way you hope to win me over, you're wrong. Dead wrong.''

He shrugged in the semidarkness, candlelight dancing across the plastered wall, creating patterns on the stone floor. ''I don't need to win you over. I already own you.''

He touched her again, this time brushing her shoulder with the tip of his finger, his fingertip gliding across her heated skin. Bryn felt a ball of desire coil in her belly, the hunger so strong it sent a rush of blood between her thighs.

"Three years I've waited for you," he continued softly. "Three years. You don't think I'm going to let you escape now?"

"Loving someone isn't about possession!"

His fingertip found her breast, slowly circled the budding nipple. "Who said anything about love? I'm thinking retribution." He tweaked her pert nipple, not gently, and she gasped. "Now sleep. I'm tired. You've made it a very long day." And with that he rolled over and closed his eyes. Within minutes his breathing changed, indicating he had really, truly fallen asleep.

Bryn stretched out her legs, her body aching, trembling, every muscle tight and unsatisfied. There was a special hell for men like Kahlil and Bryn wished her husband there with every beat of her heart.

Later, much later, a sinfully delicious warmth stole over her and she stirred, although only a little, unwilling to lose the pleasure. She felt wonderful, her skin felt wonderful, her body sensitive and alive. *Sleep or dream?* she asked herself, giving over to the heat and pleasure, not wanting to open her eyes in case it was just a dream.

Hands slid across her middle, over her breasts, a knee parting her own.

This was no dream. Immediately she remembered where she was, who she was with, and eyes flying open she gazed into Kahlil's gold eyes. The candles had burned low, most having extinguished themselves, and Kahlil's face was heavily shadowed.

He cupped her breast, his rough palm grazing her nipple and her lips parted, first a protest, and then a sigh.

Helplessly she arched her back, as her body stirred to life. She lifted her lashes to stare at his mouth, longing to be kissed by him again, wanting his lips against hers.

Kahlil shifted, kicking aside the satin sheet, his strong, naked thigh planting between her knees, parting her legs and moving between her thighs.

Her nightgown hiked up, tangling around her hips. She wanted nothing more than to circle his neck with her arms and draw his head down to hers. She craved his mouth, his tongue, his touch.

But instead of covering her mouth, his lips found the sensitive places on her neck, secret nerve endings that responded only to him. His tongue circled from earlobe to collarbone and she breathed faster, shallowly, head spinning with the dizzy pleasure.

Bryn worked her arms free and immediately wrapped her arms around his shoulders. They were broad, and she held him as if she were drowning. Being this close to him, being celibate so long, unleashed powerful emotions that had nothing to do with mere physical desire.

She needed him—needed to be a part of him, loved by him the way only he could love her.

"You're on fire," he whispered, his voice husky.

"I need you."

He didn't need any other encouragement. Impatiently Kahlil stripped her of her panties and slid his palm up the inside of her thigh, setting off a riot of sensation. Every place he touched burned, her skin glowing hot, then cold and hot again.

She trembled, waiting for his touch, knowing he'd touch her intimately and when he did, it would be intense, and intensely erotic.

At last his fingers cupped her mound, pressing against her heat before parting her to discover her softness and moisture. Bryn bucked, her body tense, her nerves straining. She was too excited, too aroused, finding the gentleness of his touch as painful as it was exciting.

"Please, please—" she begged, inarticulate, her brain clouded and unable to think. All she knew was that she'd waited forever to be with him, she had dreamed of him, dreamed of this night after night, year after year, and to finally be with him and not part of him… *"Kahlil."*

"Patience," he answered, easing his hand in her, over her, awakening her again, pushing her to a brittle brink.

Bryn clasped his ribs, lifting her mouth to his chest, holding him hard and close, as if she could melt into him, become one with him, escape the limitations of skin and bone.

She felt him harden, his arousal more ardent, his body tensing. She felt a smile inside of her, enjoying her own brief glimpse of power, and parting her lips, she kissed his chest, tongue teasing across the ridge of muscle, down the breastbone and across to one contracted nipple.

Subtle spice filled her nose, his warm skin fragrant, his body deliciously put together. Sucking his nipple, she heard him groan. Her small smile became a thrill of pleasure. She was exultant that she could make him ache, make him feel, make him reach for her.

His pleasure fed hers, shooting hot darts of sensation from her breast to her belly, her lower abdomen tight and heavy. She needed him inside her now.

Bryn wrapped her hands around his back and dragged him closer. She felt his erection brush against her sensitive folds. "Now, Kahlil, please."

He moved, parting her knees wider, sliding her feet up to create more tension. The gold chain swinging between them clinked, rattling, a stark reminder of the bitter ties binding them.

Kahlil frowned, his features dark, his expression forbidding. She felt his tension, felt the anticipation, but realized with a glance at his narrowed eyes and thin-lipped mouth that he would take her but not love her.

And still she wanted him.

Clasping her bottom, he lifted her hips higher, hesitating just a second before driving deep inside her. This was no gentle lovemaking but a statement of ownership. He was branding her his with each hard, penetrating thrust. He filled her completely, her body tender, tight stretching to accept him. She felt like a virgin, inexperienced and overwhelmed by his strength and driving passion.

She couldn't catch her breath, couldn't hold his shoulders, kiss his lips. He was taking her his way, filling her, dominating her, and she shuddered beneath him as his hips rocked against her, each deep thrust felt more raw, more intense, more powerful than the last. She felt alive, too alive, her skin, her bones, her muscles tightening, tensing, every nerve ending concentrating. Suddenly it was too strong, too real, the flood of emotion rising swiftly within her made her oblivious to all but this razor-sharp sensation.

Kahlil arched into her, straining, pushing her to the surface. That last thrust threw her from control into the wild beyond. She would have screamed if his mouth hadn't covered hers, sucking the brilliant pleasure from her lips into his mouth.

She felt utterly lost, shudder after shudder coursing through her, tears filling her eyes. She'd wanted him, she needed him…she would always need him. She could never deny him anything. Not even her heart.

Kahlil sighed, a sound of pure exasperation and Bryn felt his reluctance as he drew her close to him, forming a safe, protective circle around her with his arms.

Yet he didn't say a word. And he gave no other caress.

Tears stung the back of her eyes and she bit her lower lip, fighting to hang on to her last vestige of pride. They'd made love many, many times before, but it had never felt so empty afterward, never so naked and needy and…desperate.

Bryn longed to grab the sheet and cover them, or find a corner and hide, but the handcuff chafed her wrist, a heavy reminder that she was tied to him.

# CHAPTER SEVEN

"Last night was a mistake." Kahlil wouldn't even look at her, his back turned to her, his shadow stretching long across the sunlit courtyard. "It can't happen again, and it won't. From now on you will sleep in the women's quarters, even if I must chain you to the floor."

Making love last night had only increased the tension between them. Anger crackled from him in invisible electric waves. "You don't have to chain me to the floor. You have Ben. I'm not going anywhere."

"As if I trust anything you say."

Bryn ignored his contemptuous snort, keeping her own emotions carefully checked. It had been painful last night to be in Kahlil's bed. Realizing too late that she hadn't sufficiently hardened her heart had done nothing to assuage the aching emptiness in her heart. If this was love, she could live without it.

"You don't trust me, but you'll make love to me."

"I'm sorry. I lost control. I'll do my best to make sure it never happens again."

If he was trying to hurt her, he was succeeding. Chaining her to him wasn't punishment enough. He'd degrade her now. Humiliate her after sharing the most intimate act of all. Pain splintered within her, fresh realization at the depth of his hatred for her. "Well, I won't apologize. What happened between us was lovely.''

''It was sex.''

Her cheeks burned, heat surging to her face. She wouldn't back down. Refused to let him turn their love-making into something ugly and sordid. She'd been a willing partner last night. And so had he. ''Then it was good sex, great sex.''

He cast her a dubious glance over his shoulders, lips twisting grimly. ''You speak for me, or just yourself?''

A second surge of blood followed the first. *Stand firm,* she seethed. *Don't roll over and die.* ''Why not? You said we're still married, so why shouldn't we find comfort in each other's arms?''

''I find no comfort in sleeping with you. Just release.''

She'd vowed not to cry, and she'd meant to keep her vow, but his harshness hurt, cutting deep. She ached at the change in him, the change in them. She couldn't do this, she couldn't stay frozen emotionally. Not when he was making her feel so much and reminding her of how things had been.

Years ago when they made love, he'd murmur endearments in his native tongue, *Sweet flower of the garden; most beautiful night star; treasure of the desert.* No longer. His hatred was palpable.

If she didn't have Ben, she might have run from his anger, but she couldn't run. She needed to win Kahlil's trust, and custody of Ben. Ben needed his daddy, and she needed Kahlil, too.

Heartache gave way to action. Bryn stiffened, her

shoulders squaring. She'd do what she had to do. She'd make her marriage work, by hell or high water.

By hell or high water, she repeated silently, fiercely.

No regrets. No turning back. "Tell me what you want from me. I shall do whatever you wish. I shall be exactly as you want me to be."

"Such a change of heart."

"It's the conviction of my heart."

"You do this for me?"

"And my son."

"Ah, your son." His smile was flinty, his gold eyes icy. "I wondered when you'd return to that theme. This isn't about me, is it? It's about you, and you getting your way."

"I just want to see Ben. Even if it's just for a few minutes."

"You're in no position to make demands."

"I realize that. I'm prepared to bargain."

"Bargain or beg?"

"Either," she answered wearily. "I'll do anything to see him."

"Anything?"

The coldness in his voice stole her breath but she held her position, hands pressing together for courage. He'd push her, she realized, push her to the brink and beyond. "Anything." She clung to her resolve. It was all she had left. "I will accept whatever punishment you give me, and I will serve you in whatever capacity you request, provided you let me see my son. Soon."

"We'll see."

"Does that mean I might be able to see him today, or tonight?"

"It means I'm thinking about it."

It didn't answer the burning loneliness. "I need to know he's okay."

"He is fine."

"I don't know what fine means."

"I do, and I tell you he's fine."

"Not good enough!"

"It's all the reassurance you're getting."

She shivered inwardly, hurting in ways he couldn't imagine. He hadn't known Ben long enough to feel the intense and desperate need to love and protect one's child. Every nerve in her body screamed to bridge the distance between her and Ben, every muscle ached to just hold him against her chest. It was such a primitive instinct, but truer than anything else she'd ever felt. "Tell me what you want me to do, Kahlil, and I shall do it."

"There's nothing you can do."

"Don't say that, there must be a task, give me one, let's think of one."

"*Baraka!* Stop."

Bryn felt as though she was losing control, her emotions dangerously unhinged. "Let me prove myself, let me prove I can be trusted." She fell to her knees and clasped her hands, begging. "I will serve you, obey you—"

Kahlil hauled her to her feet, scorn blazing in his eyes. "How can I respect you, if you insist on behaving like a madwoman? I did not marry you for this, I do not desire a wife without control—''

''But you've reduced me to this! To begging, groveling, pleading. I am yours. I am no better than your handmaidens in the harem. I will do whatever I must to please you. Now let me prove it.''

A tiny muscle in his jaw popped. He reached inside his outer robe, drawing papers from a pocket sewn on the inside. ''Then sign it. Let's get this over with.''

Her fingers curled into her palm. She didn't dare touch the papers, viewing them as something inherently offensive. ''What are those?''

''Divorce papers.''

His voice shivered down her spine, his tone incredibly cold and unfeeling.

''I've been advised by my cabinet to move forward with the divorce,'' he continued. ''I've lost too much face with my people. My staff and servants know I cannot manage you. Word has spread about your disloyalty and there is no place for you here anymore.''

She didn't speak, didn't trust herself to answer. After last night, after the passion in his bed…he'd do this?

He edged towards her, the papers rustling in his hand. ''I will take care of you financially, of course.''

Chilled from head to toe, Bryn wrapped her arms around herself, gold bracelets tinkling like water splashing from the fountain. ''And Ben?'' Her voice sounded like a flutter, a whisper of wings on the sun-kissed morning.

''He'd remain with me.''

Of course.

"Sign them," Kahlil ruthlessly continued, "and by this afternoon you'll be on a plane home. Free."

Bryn heard a faint, dull buzz in her head, rather like the hum of a vacuum. She gave her head a slow shake to dislodge the buzzing noise. "Won't sign that. Ever."

"It's in your best interest."

"No, *it's in yours.*" She felt warmth bead her brow, her body growing hot where moments ago it had been cold. "What kind of mother do you think I am, to turn my back on my child?"

"I'd arrange visits."

"Unacceptable."

"Mothers do it all the time."

"Not this one. Not ever."

"The child would adjust, better than you think."

*"The child."* Fury rocketed through her. She clenched her hands, resisting the urge to lash out at him, physically and emotionally. "Not *the child,* but Ben. Your son, my son, our son. I won't leave here without Ben."

"And I won't let him go."

"Then I stay." Shaking, she grabbed the documents from his hand, tearing them into little bits before he could stop her. "I'll never divorce you. If you want to keep him here, then you keep me as well. It's a package deal, Kahlil. Ben and I stay together, always."

She'd rendered him speechless. Good! Because anything he said just now would seriously push her over the edge.

The strained silence enveloped them in a cloak of

quiet that stilled the distant chirping of birds and splash of fountain.

When Kahlil finally broke the silence, his voice was quiet, almost thoughtful. "Always?"

"Yes."

"You'd do that for your son?"

He knew so little about the power of love! The papers scattered from her fingers and she threw her head back, the sun dazzling her, blinding her eyes. She couldn't see him clearly, only felt him, huge and overpowering. "I would die for him. In a heartbeat."

"Just like that?"

"No question in my mind. Is that what you want me to do? Pay the ultimate sacrifice?"

"God, no!" Kahlil visibly drew back, his expression closing, lashes lowering. He turned away to gaze across the protected courtyard. "How far we've come from what we were."

His voice, a mere whisper, wafted in the warm sunlight, wound its way into the tenderness of her heart. *How far we've come from what we were.*

Was that really regret she heard? Was that sorrow she saw in his eyes?

Her own eyes burned and a knot formed in her throat.

Kahlil turned his back to her. "I think it's best if you returned to your quarters. We'll talk later. I promise."

It wasn't the way he'd planned the meeting. He'd expected tears, yes, and angry accusations, but not her willingness to beg—beg!—at his feet, to kneel before him and offer herself, a sacrifice at the altar.

His gut burned, his eyes burned, his heart burned. Fire in his chest. Fire in his head. Fire everywhere. Kahlil swallowed with difficulty, his mouth tasting sour. He found no pleasure in his victory, no joy in his power, especially after what had taken place between them the night before. He'd wanted her, needed to feel her, touch her, taste her, but his desire infuriated him.

How could he want a woman he didn't trust? How could he desire her when she'd betrayed him both privately and publicly, breaking every sacred vow?

He'd wanted to punish her this morning, force her to submit, and yet when she did…it made him even angrier.

Kahlil slumped against the marble pillar, his head aching, his temper barely leashed. He was furious, but tonight his anger was directed entirely at himself.

Bryn had never been like the other women he'd taken to bed. From the beginning she was different, exciting, innocent, passionate, daring. She'd wanted the world and he'd been eager to give it to her. He'd thought he could give it to her. He'd failed.

A knock sounded on the outer door of his chamber. Kahlil called out, knowing it was his valet, and welcomed Rifaat to enter.

''The new papers,'' Rifaat said, walking the documents to Kahlil's large ornate desk in the center of the room and setting them down. ''They just need your signature.''

Perplexed, Kahlil stared at the sheath on his desk. He

knew what his advisors had suggested but he wasn't sure he could follow through with it. "Thank you."

"I suppose you could force her to sign."

Force, there it was again. Force her to submit, force her to bed, force her to break. The use and abuse of his position disgusted him. Why didn't revenge taste sweeter? Why didn't he relish his power? "She won't leave Ben."

The valet didn't answer and Kahlil pushed off the pillar and approached the desk, lifting the documents to read them yet again. "At least she's a better mother than a wife."

Still, Rifaat said nothing.

Wearily Kahlil tossed the papers back onto the gleaming surface of the desk. "Has my cousin arrived yet?"

"No."

"Let me know when he does. Good night."

"Good night, my lord."

Kahlil crouched next to the small bed in the nursery and gently drew the covers back. The child stirred, curling his hand more closely beneath his cheek, nestling deeper into his pillow.

*Little boy, my boy.* Kahlil's eyes burned, and with a hard swallow, he accepted that it could not continue like this. It would not continue like this. There ought to be a sanctuary for children, a sacred place to protect their innocence. Their tenderness.

Perhaps if he had been protected as a child he might be a different man today...he might be a different leader.

Kahlil's palm rested against his son's head. The child's hair felt silky, his scalp felt warm. Kahlil could feel his son breathe, feel his son's innate strength.

*Protect the child. Protect his life.*

Calmer, feeling the first hint of peace in days, Kahlil scooped Ben into his arms and stood. The boy weighed nothing but meant everything.

Footsteps sounded in her room. Bryn lifted her head, squinting in the darkness as her heart raced. Someone was in her room. Someone was moving her way.

She swung her legs out from beneath the covers and rubbed her eyes. Full of fear she was reminded of another night, another intruder.

"Bryn."

Kahlil.

Her husband's deep voice, his English crisp, formal, echoed in the dark. "Are you awake?"

"Yes. What's happened?"

"Nothing. Shh, he's still asleep. Don't wake him."

Suddenly she knew. Bryn nearly lunged from bed, flinging the covers back. Kahlil had brought Ben back to her!

Kahlil placed Ben on the mattress next to her and drew the silk comforter up, covering them. Speechless, Bryn pressed the back of her hand to Ben's warm cheek. He was real. He was here.

Warmth filled her. A dizzying hope. "Thank you," she choked, the words grossly inadequate. "Thank you so much."

Kahlil nodded, and without speaking, headed for the door.

"Kahlil, what does this mean?"

Her voice stopped him. "I don't know." He hesitated, his features shadowed, his expression reserved. "Maybe it means we call a truce. No more fighting. At least, not over our son."

"Never again," she swiftly agreed. "Kahlil, thank you again. I mean it. From the bottom of my heart—"

"I know."

He stood framed in the doorway, the soft yellow light of the hall illuminating his height and strength and his honey-gold skin.

He looked like a prince from a medieval storybook, darkly handsome and yet so alone. She realized bleakly that he had no one, not since she had left him.

He hesitated in the doorway. She felt his tension, his silence throbbing with unspoken meaning.

The ache in her chest was so strong it made it nearly impossible to breathe. She wanted to go to him, touch him, hold him, love him. But she was afraid, so afraid of the distance between them.

"Good night, Bryn. I hope you sleep well."

"I will now."

"So will I." He turned, and left, heading off alone into the dark of the night.

Bryn cuddled Ben to her but she couldn't sleep. Minutes passed, a half hour crept by, and then finally an hour, but it wasn't a peaceful rest. She felt anything but peaceful, not when Kahlil punctuated her thoughts.

From the moment she ran into Kahlil in the Dallas parking lot, she'd felt the impact of the fender-bender accident reverberate through every part of her life.

When Kahlil climbed out of his luxury sedan, the shock wave deepened. He had said words that her mind didn't capture. She couldn't focus on his speech, only on his face. She'd known him sometime, somewhere. Recognized him from a previous life. She couldn't tear her gaze away. Entranced by the symmetry of his brow, sweep of cheekbone, the strong aquiline nose, he was the most amazing man she'd ever seen. Like Valentino from the old movies, he seemed perfect.

Kahlil had been astonished that she not only knew where Tiva was, but that she'd spent her first thirteen years in the Middle East, most in the Zwar desert. They'd gone for coffee and the one coffee became an all-night conversation.

Disarmingly honest, he told her she wasn't like most women in his country. She'd thought he meant it as a compliment. Now she knew better. Their cultural differences would destroy them, if she let it.

Kahlil needed her, but he'd never tell her. Not after she'd betrayed him, and she had betrayed him. She'd become too close to Amin, developing a friendship with an Arab man—Kahlil's first cousin, of all people!—to answer her insecurity. It hadn't been enough to be loved by Kahlil. She'd needed endless reassurance, constant proof of love.

Bryn wanted to blame her insecurity on her parents' death, and the culture shock she'd experienced moving to Aunt Rose's house in Texas, but she'd felt adrift before the market blast. Truthfully she felt adrift most of her life. She'd never felt at ease with her parents' nomadic lifestyle, nor their ability to live without friends, and worldly possessions. She wanted a bedroom of her own, pink rosebud paper on the walls, chintz curtains, lots of dolls and stuffed animals on her pillow. She wanted books on shelves, toys stacked in a closet, shoes and clothes tucked in a solid wood dresser.

Instead there had been one knapsack, a half-dozen worn dresses, a battered brown bear. Her parents meant well. They believed they were an example of good values, teaching her that things didn't matter, making it clear that too many possessions only tied one down. But Bryn wanted to be tied down and longed for the stability of a real house. It was her great childhood fantasy, waking up to discover her parents had bought a two-story house with shingles and shutters and a painted picket fence. There would be kids riding bikes on the street, and girls jumping rope or playing jacks. Bryn would go to a real school and every day she would walk home, carrying her book bag and laughing with her schoolmates.

Her parents laughed at her fantasy world, telling her it was the exact thing they'd left behind. No ordinary life for them.

Bryn had spent most of her life trying to be ordinary. Kahlil had not been ordinary. But he'd wanted what she did—stability, security, tradition. And family. They both wanted children. Desperately.

Bryn gently kissed Ben, careful not to wake him. She was grateful to hold him again, soothed by his proximity. But she couldn't sleep, not when her thoughts revolved around Kahlil.

Tonight, for the first time in years, she'd seen a chink in Kahlil's armor, and instead of moving in to wound him, she wanted only to protect him. Protect the man she'd once loved, *still loved,* when he was at his most vulnerable.

She felt a tumult of emotion, even new emotions, a combination of tenderness…forgiveness…regret. Once she and Kahlil had been so sweet together, so full of hope and love. Could they find it again? Could they ever find their way back to each other again?

Bryn slid out of bed, leaving Ben nestled in her pillows and covers, and rang for her maid. She explained that she needed to be taken to Kahlil immediately.

He was in bed, sleeping. Rifaat opened the door for her, giving her access where all else would be denied.

Bryn hadn't stopped to think, she just acted, responding to the impulse that drove her from her room to his in the dead of night.

Kahlil sat up, the satin sheet falling to his waist. Her heart did a funny double-beat. He looked shockingly sexual. Breathtakingly male, and virile.

Unlike Stan.

Unlike any other man she'd ever known.

Kahlil's gold eyes, heavily lashed and darkly brooding, met hers. ''Yes?''

As their gazes locked her heart turned over. His eyes

undid her. She wanted only to go to him, beg him to forgive her, beg him to love her. Instead she stood stiffly several feet away, feeling the chasm between them, the secrets and mistrust, the mistakes and fear.

He shifted restlessly. ''What do you want?''

Her chest constricted. ''You.''

Kahlil's forehead furrowed, an ebony lock shadowing his strong, beautiful face. Slowly he flipped back the satin sheet, making space for her next to him. It was the same thing she'd done earlier for Ben.

She ran to him, climbed into his bed, burying herself in his arms. ''Kahlil, I—''

He stopped her, silencing her words with his lips. 'No,'' he whispered. ''No talking, I don't trust words.''

His lips covered hers, and his body moved against her, the hard planes of his chest brushing the peaks of her aching breasts, his hips pressing to her belly. She felt him harden, and he moved her onto her back, his weight braced on his elbows. Fire surged within her, fire and hunger. Only one man could answer this feverish need, and that man was her first and last love, Kahlil.

# CHAPTER EIGHT

SKIN still damp, desire finally satiated, Bryn gazed up at Kahlil, waiting for him to speak. She knew there was something on his mind. He had that look, the tension at his mouth, fine creases fanning from his eyes.

She wouldn't press the issue, if there was an issue. Far better to give Kahlil time. And truly, she felt deliciously relaxed, muscles weak, pulse finally slowing from its earlier furious rhythm.

Kahlil reached for her, running his callused palm across her bare midriff, over her rib cage, his fingers exploring each rib and inch of skin until he cupped one breast, and its rose-tipped peak in his hand. ''You were serious yesterday, about staying?''

She stared at his hand on her breast, torn between the warmth stealing through her, the heat surging to life yet again in her belly and between her thighs, and the fear his words created.

''Bryn?''

He still wanted to send her home. Even after this, after the most intimate acts a man and woman could do together.

She closed her eyes briefly. ''I won't go, if that's what you're asking.''

''Is that what I'm asking?'' He kicked back the sheet,

exposing both of them to light. His body was hard everywhere, his chest deep, hips narrow and hard, his thigh thickly muscled. He was still so strong. She could see the soldier in him. He'd served six years in the Zwar military. All Zwar men served their country. Ben would have to serve as well.

"Well, isn't it?" she returned, unconsciously squaring her shoulders, denying her desire to feel him again, be taken again, savored again. He made her feel like a delicacy and she loved his skill, his incredible sexual prowess.

But that wasn't the issue, she reminded herself, wondering why she'd though Kahlil would ever be anything but an adversary. Truce, indeed! He was still trying to wrest Ben from her custody. "Ben and I stay together. Always."

"No divorce?"

"Not a chance."

Abruptly Kahlil leaned forward and suckled one of her nipples. Silvery arrows of sensation shot from her nipple to her belly and she moaned a protest.

Kahlil lifted his head, smiled his satisfaction. He relished his power over her. Relished the control. "So you have no objection then to renewing our vows?"

*Renewing vows.* Bryn jerked, grabbed for the sheet, feeling the need for protection. "Renew vows...as in *marry* again?"

He pushed her hand away from the sheet. "Leave it. I like seeing you this way."

"I can't think naked."

"Of course you can. Concentrate." His gaze turned brooding. "We were married the first time in an American courthouse. This time we'd do it here. A traditional Arab ceremony."

Marry Kahlil again?

Her mind spun, thoughts racing, her body felt heavy, almost languid.

To be loved by Kahlil again, feel the strength and hunger of his passion not just once, but again and again, to return to his arms, his heart, his—

But he wasn't declaring love. She wasn't returning as a beloved wife, but as an object. His property. This was part of his domination, his need for control.

So? A little voice challenged deep inside her. What did it matter? She'd be with him; they'd be a family. Ben would have what he wanted and Bryn—she'd be with Kahlil again, and really, wasn't that what she wanted?

There was no reason they couldn't make it work. It had been wonderful between them in the beginning, heaven, sweet heaven before the worst hell.

A clock bonged somewhere in the palace. She felt the weight of time, the weight of the past. The last three and a half years had been so long, so incredibly difficult. She couldn't imagine going back to that kind of life again. "If we were never divorced, why do we need to renew our vows?"

He reached out, plucked a long white-gold tendril from her shoulder, and allowed the hair to slip between his fingers. "It's a show of faith."

The intimacy of the touch, the ease with which he touched her, created a hunger inside of her, her belly tightening with need. If only he'd touch her again, her cheek, her breast, her belly, her thighs. She sucked in a breath, appalled by the intensity of her desire.

"Is this for Ben's b…benefit?" she asked, curling her fingers into her palms, her limbs melting, her body melting.

"Ben, and my people."

His people. But not her. Never her.

It stung, but better that he be honest than let her get her hopes up. This way she knew where she stood. This time she was not the beloved, but the obligation. Not the jewel in his crown but the mother of his son.

Kahlil caught her chin in his fingers and turned her head to face him. "You have a problem marrying me again?"

"No." She could see nothing now but Kahlil's face. Her gaze met his and she stared into his eyes, mesmerized by gold flecks and the determination she saw there. He exuded intensity, and conviction. He was brilliant, complex, emotional. He fascinated her mind and confounded her heart.

Leaning forward Kahlil's nose briefly touched hers, his lips a breath away. "You must be quite sure, Bryn. I won't suffer a runaway wife again."

His lips brushed hers. A shiver raced down her spine.

"Hmm?" he murmured, his fingers splaying against her jaw, his palm cool and strong against her throat.

She pressed her trembling lips to his. She was unable

to hold his words in her mind; her brain was lost to hunger.

His mouth, firm, cool, rasped her lips. He drew back an inch. "I need an answer, Bryn."

Her eyes closed. She leaned forward a hair, closing the distance between them again. "Yes."

"You'll marry me again?"

"Yes."

And this time when they made love it was with hunger and intensity, a consuming desire that nearly burned them both alive. Nothing mattered, she thought blindly, nothing mattered but them, and this.

She returned to her room just before dawn, senses satiated, heart still raw. She was wrong, she acknowledged, opening her door and gazing at sleeping Ben, there were things that did matter more than making love to Kahlil.

Ben, for starters.

And earning Kahlil's love.

All the lovemaking in the world wasn't enough to ease the loneliness inside her. Kahlil touched her, tasted her, took her with passion but the emptiness in her heart, the detachment in his expression, only grew.

If only he'd utter one affectionate word, give her a sign of deeper feelings, but he kept his emotions hidden and shared with her just...skin.

His body. Her body. He was doing his best to reduce their relationship to sex.

Bryn closed her eyes, leaned against the doorframe, drawing a slow, ragged breath. She wanted Kahlil, but she wanted it the way it had once been between them. She wanted Kahlil to love her. And he didn't.

Her fear, at first small, but now growing, was that he wouldn't. Ever. But she clamped down on the fear, reducing it in size until she could breathe easier. She refused to panic, had no intention of subjecting herself—or Ben—to emotional chaos. Once she might have run away from her fears, but not anymore.

Bryn bathed and was dressed by the time Ben awoke. His delight in seeing her brought tears to her eyes. He hugged her and hugged her, holding so tightly she begged him to be gentle, to let her breathe.

"I love Mommy, I love you!"

"I love you. I missed you." She kissed his mouth, his forehead, the tip of his nose. "How are you? What have you been doing?"

He told her about his activities, chattering as she dressed him and continuing through breakfast, talking a mile a minute about everything he'd discovered since arriving in Zwar. Puppies, and miniature trains, cousins, soccer and card games. Lots to eat. Movies on videotape. Even a ride on a beautiful black pony.

"You've done all that in only two days?" Bryn said, indulgently teasing him, enjoying every breathless announcement he made.

They lingered over their breakfast in the courtyard, Ben frequently leaving his chair to creep into her lap for a snuggle.

Now with the dishes cleared away he'd begun to explore the patio garden, first poking at a pill bug he'd discovered in one of the massive clay pots and then sniffing at gardenias planted beneath a tall palm.

Footsteps echoed on the stone floor. Bryn glanced up, hoping it was Lalia with the promised coffee. Bryn had found the adjustment to mint tea impossible, but it wasn't Lalia with coffee.

It was a man. Broad-shouldered, slim-hipped, darkly handsome like Kahlil but not as tall. Amin stood before her in an expensive light gray suit, white shirt, pewter silk tie smiling. "Hello, gorgeous."

Bryn's arm went nerveless, her hand falling to her lap. She tried to stand but couldn't. "What are you doing here?"

"Is that the welcome I get after all these years?" Amin thrust a hand into his trouser pockets, head bending, dark hair cut close, accenting his beauty. And he was beautiful, more so than Kahlil, the beauty of Hollywood film stars, fine bones, perfect symmetry in his features. But now his elegance and polish repelled Bryn. His external beauty hid the heart of a snake.

"You have no business being here."

"But I live here." He smiled. A thin, flat, hard smile.

"Not in this part of the palace. These are my private rooms, part of the women's quarters." Although that didn't stop him last time.

Amin's smooth handsome face creased before quickly clearing. He lifted a hand, gesturing to the sun and sky. "We're outside, and all this belongs to Allah."

Finally her legs found the strength and she pushed up

from her chair, glancing in Ben's direction where he'd followed a ladybug beneath the breakfast table. "Then we shall go inside."

"I'm surprised you're not happier to see me. We have…unfinished business."

She stiffened, her gaze locking on the curve of Ben's small back, the shape of his hand as he prodded the spotted ladybug into flight. "There is no business between us, and I will not let you ruin my life again."

Amin followed her gaze, his heavily lashed eyes narrowing as he focused on Ben. "A handsome child." He drew aside the lace tablecloth. "He looks rather like me."

Her breath caught in her throat. She couldn't believe Amin had the gall to say such a thing. "I don't see the resemblance."

But Amin was grasping Ben by the shoulders and lifting him to his feet. Bryn's heart leaped in her chest. It made her skin crawl seeing Amin put his hands on her son.

"It's there in the eyes," Amin said, roughly tilting Ben's head back, before twisting his head one way and then the other. "His nose and mouth, like mine. He could be mine, couldn't he?"

Meet fire with fire, she told herself, resisting the urge to grab Ben and run. "It's only natural for you to see a family likeness." Reaching for Ben, she firmly drew him away from Amin against her own body, shielding him within the circle of her arms. "As Sheikh al-Assad's first cousin you have many of the same characteristics."

"Yes, his first cousin." Amin's eyes glittered like ice. "How lucky we are to have each other."

"Luckier than you deserve."

"You really shouldn't take that tone with me," he drawled, taking seat in the chair opposite the one she'd just vacated. He stretched out his legs and crossed his arms behind his head, revealing his solid gold Rolex watch. "I take it you've never told him about us."

"There is no 'us,'" she answered sharply. "Never has been."

"Darling Bryn, how can you say that? We were once quite close." His lips pursed, eyebrows rising suggestively. "*Very, very* close."

"Not that close."

"You invited me to your room."

She had, but not like that. Not the way he was making it sound. Hand shaking she reached for Ben, needing to touch him, needing to find strength. "You know I only wanted to talk."

"Do I?"

She felt sick, dreadfully sick, the realization that this was one nightmare that wouldn't end. Amin was evil, the worst kind of evil, and she didn't know how to deal with him.

"I'm taking my son inside." She clasped Ben's hand in hers and squeezed it, fearing for him, for her, for Kahlil. If she let him, Amin would destroy everything again.

"Darling, you can run, but you can't hide." Amin's

perfect English followed her. "I'm back, and I'm waiting."

Bryn pushed Ben inside the door to her bedchamber, and locked it, before sinking to the ground and covering her face with her hands. She felt hot and cold and violently ill. *Please God, no, don't let him do this to me again...*

Small hands pulled her own away from her face. "Mommy?"

Bryn heard his voice, saw his face but felt such unspeakable horror and dread that she could only manage the briefest of smiles, her lips stiff, unyielding. "It's okay, baby."

But it wasn't okay. It was anything but okay.

"You can't go in there now—"

Bryn brushed past Rifaat, throwing open the doors to the suite of rooms that housed the palace office. Computers, huge color monitors, phones, faxes, file cabinets, security cameras...the office came equipped, no old world palace in this modern suite.

Two secretaries startled, covered heads lifting from their keyboards. A third assistant appeared from an inner office. All stared at Bryn.

She didn't care. "Where is he?" she demanded, her gaze sweeping the dark paneled walls, deep red Persian carpet, the massive oil painting depicting a feudal warlord sacking a walled city while horrified people ran from burning buildings.

"He's on a conference call," Rifaat answered sharply, placing his body between hers and a partially open door.

Rifaat's heroic measures were unnecessary. Kahlil, dressed in Western clothes, black turtleneck and olive-green check trousers, appeared immediately in the inner office doorway, his broad shoulders filling the narrow space.

''What's going on in here?'' He held a cordless phone to his chest. His black hair was ruffled, and his deep voice crackled with impatience.

''Nice painting,'' she snapped, furious with Amin, Rifaat, Kahlil, all of them. She'd forgotten the politics of the palace, the sheer implausibility of getting anything accomplished...at least if you were a woman.

''You interrupted an OPEC meeting to talk about my painting?''

''No.'' She drew a deep breath, her confidence suddenly flagging. ''Your cousin Amin is back.''

''Yes, I know, and he told me he saw you in the garden today.'' Kahlil's brows drew together. ''He said you chatted for a few minutes and introduced Ben. Is there a problem?''

The way he put it, the visit between her and Amin sounded quite amicable. He wanted it to be amicable. Amin was his cousin after all, one of his closest relations. ''No,'' she faltered, ''I just wasn't sure you knew he'd returned.''

''You're pleased then? He reminded me that you two were once such good friends.''

She felt sick, her skin clammy. Trust Amin to begin planting poisonous seeds! She struggled to think of something that wouldn't be incriminating. She wasn't ready to tell Kahlil about Amin's assault. She needed to think of a way to share with him her own weaknesses and failings first. "I…yes, it's always a pleasure to see your family. I just wished you had been the one to introduce Ben."

"We'll have dinner tonight. I'll make sure he joins us. Ben, too. I'll take care of formal introductions then."

Alarm bells sounded in her head. She wouldn't expose Ben to Amin again. She could handle Amin, as long as Ben wasn't present, subjected to Kahlil's cousin's cruelty and games. "I know you like to eat late. It's really too late for a little boy. What if just the three of us had dinner? Better yet, maybe you and Amin would prefer to have dinner alone tonight."

"The three of us," Kahlil said firmly. "It wouldn't be a celebration without you."

Anxiety tangled her in knots. "What are we celebrating?"

"All of us being together again. Just like old times."

Lalia formed a crown on Bryn's head of silvery-blond ringlets, the blond strands smooth, gleaming with a scented pomade. She dressed her in a slim white gown with a plunging neckline, which was more daring than most and a narrow silk skirt beaded with hundreds of tiny seed pearls.

"You look like a queen," Lalia said admiringly, handing Bryn a mirror.

But gazing at her reflection, Bryn didn't see a queen— she saw her worry, her eyes wide, anxious, her forehead knit, her lips pressed so tightly that white lines etched on either side of her pink mouth.

She was to meet Kahlil in his dining room in half an hour. But she had to speak to him first, before Amin appeared.

Bryn appeared at Kahlil's bedroom door without invitation. He frowned at her sudden appearance but didn't rebuke her. Yet his expression darkened when she mentioned she'd rather have a quiet dinner with him without Amin being present.

"You object to my cousin?" he asked shortly, tightening the black-and-gold belt worn over his white crisp trousers, and casting a narrowed glance in her direction.

"I'm more comfortable alone with you." She squirmed at her inability to be more direct. She wanted to tell him about Amin, but needed to approach the subject carefully. She needed Kahlil's trust, first, and a stronger bond.

"But I've already asked him to join us. It would be impolite to break the engagement now. That is, unless there's a reason why he shouldn't be included." Kahlil paused, a pregnant silence. "Bryn?"

She shifted uneasily, wondering if this was some kind of a test. What did Kahlil want her to say? "I…I'm not feeling very sociable tonight, that's all."

"But you look beautiful."

The compliment was edged with savagery. Bryn swallowed nervously. Something wasn't right. Kahlil didn't seem himself, or at least, not like the man she'd woken up with this morning.

"Amin's on his way to the dining hall now. What am I to tell him?" Kahlil persisted, sliding his arms into his outer robe. "That I've changed my mind? That I'd prefer

an intimate meal with my wife instead of dinner together?''

''You are the sheikh,'' she whispered.

But he didn't immediately reply, just watched her with
the same hawklike wariness he revealed earlier. ''All
right. Fine. I'll send word that you and I are to dine
alone, but I can't get out of the evening completely. I'll
invite him for an hour from now. He'll have coffee and
dessert with us.''

It was better than nothing. And perhaps by some miracle, she'd find a way in the next hour to tell Kahlil
exactly what had happened all those years ago.

Grilled marinated lamb, peppers, saffron rice. The meal
was simple and yet delicious. They sat facing each other
on the carpeted floor, pillows behind their backs, a low
table placed before them. Kahlil relaxed during dinner,
talking easily, telling her stories, and continuously re-
filling their glasses with strong, burgundy-red wine.

''No more,'' she protested laughingly, when he
moved to fill her glass again. ''You'll have me doing
something silly in no time.''

''Sounds interesting,'' he answered, half reclining.
''Could I make some suggestions? I recall a very erotic
dance you did for me once. If I remember, it required
taking off your clothes, one by one.''

She blushed. ''I don't think it's wise, especially not
with your cousin coming.''

Mentioning Amin's name profoundly changed
Kahlil's mood. He nearly knocked over his gold wine
goblet in his haste to rise. ''Not a good idea,'' he curtly

agreed, moving from her to the small sitting area furnished with large overstuffed chairs upholstered in buttery leather.

Bryn rose to gather the dishes and fill the tray.

"Leave it," he ordered, sinking into one of the massive chairs, his golden gaze hooded, his expression impossible to read. "The servants will do that. You, come sit here with me."

She wiped her hands on a damp towel and moved slowly toward him. Kahlil's good mood was gone. He exuded anger, barely leashed tension. What had she said? What had she done?

She smoothed her skirt, preparing to sit in one of the leather chairs.

"Not there. Here."

Bryn hesitated uncertainly, glancing at his long, powerful legs, the ground, the circle of chairs. "Where?"

"Here," he repeated, pointing to the carpet. "At my feet."

"On my knees?"

"Yes."

Color swept through Bryn's cheeks, humiliated by the request. She didn't move. She couldn't. She stood rooted to the spot, trembling with shame and rage.

Seconds passed, long seconds passed, one after the other. She swallowed hard. A minute must have finally squeaked by.

Kahlil pointed to the carpet at his feet.

Nerves screaming in protest, she forced herself to move, walking slowly toward him and painfully lowering herself to the floor.

"Closer," he commanded.

She resisted yet again, smoldering at his imperial tone. He waited. She hesitated.

"Do you have a problem doing my bidding?" he asked softly.

"I don't know why you want me to sit on the floor when you're inviting your cousin to join us. A chair would be more appropriate, don't you think?"

"It strikes me you're more interested in pleasing Amin than in pleasing me."

"That's not so—" She broke off at the sound of footsteps echoing on polished marble.

Amin had arrived. Kahlil gestured for him to come forward.

"Please let me up," she softly pleaded.

"No." Kahlil gazed down at her, utterly expressionless. "Stay where you are."

"You're unfair."

"One more word and I shall use you as a footstool!"

Blushing furiously, she slowly sank down, her white silk skirt beaded with pearls billowing gently.

"Closer."

Blood surging from her neck to her hairline, Bryn slid forward on her knees. Kahlil pointed to the navy cushion decorated with immense gold tassels wedged between his feet. "Here."

She cast an indignant glance at the pillow. Not just at his feet, she noted, clamping her jaw tightly together, but between his feet, like a dog panting for his master. Kahlil really was taking this king role to an extreme!

Her hesitation didn't go unnoticed. Bending down,

Kahlil tapped the pillow twice, a wordless command. All in front of Amin.

It was like pouring salt in tender wounds.

Her flashing blue eyes met Kahlil's and his thick black eyebrow lifted, *I'm waiting,* he seemed to say.

His dominance mortified her. She couldn't believe he was forcing her to submit in front of Amin. Torture, that's what this was, torture.

Irritably, her temper barely controlled, she scooted forward until she finally knelt between his legs, her hands balled in her silk-covered lap.

"That's better."

"For whom?" she gritted.

"Shh," he replied, pressing a finger to her lips. "You don't want me to enforce my threat, do you? Because surely, *laeela,* you'd feel even more inelegant as a foot-stool."

Amin laughed.

My God, he laughed.

She closed her eyes, held her breath and prayed for the ground to open.

It did not.

# CHAPTER NINE

COFFEE was poured by a servant, desserts were passed, and Bryn sat during the boring conversation staring at the carpet in front of her. Amin droned on about his life in Monte Carlo: girls, cars, gambling in the glittering casinos. But finally conversation dwindled and Kahlil eventually bade Amin good-night.

As the door closed behind Amin, Bryn jumped to her feet, her legs stiff, her knees aching. "Well, that was quite impressive! Amin must be amazed by your mastery."

"Mastery of...?"

"Me," she snapped, banging her thumb into her chest.

Kahlil leaned back in his chair, tapping a finger to his lips. "Do I have mastery over you?"

"That's not my point—"

"It's exactly my point," he interrupted. "You promised me you'd change, assured me of your loyalty. Tonight was a test. I wanted to see how you'd behave around Amin."

"Did I pass?"

"Yes. Beautifully."

"Next time, tell me your intentions. I might be able to fulfil your imperial expectations."

''Why tell you? So you can play a little game, pretend to obey? *Laeela,* I don't want pretense. I want the real thing.''

''Obedience.''

''Surrender.''

She shrugged impatiently. ''I've given you my body. I've agreed to renew our vows. What else can you want? What other proof do you need?''

''Yet you're angry.''

''Yes, I'm angry. I'm angry you think so little of me that you find it necessary to make me sit there like a lapdog, panting at your feet.''

His golden eyes suddenly gleamed, otherwise his expression remained neutral. ''One wouldn't have known you objected to my attentions—''

''*In*attention.'' She interrupted, correcting him with a scowl. ''I wasn't part of the conversation. You didn't once look at me.''

He reached out, caught her hands in his, brought one wrist to his lips, kissing the tender skin on the inside. ''I'm paying attention to you now.''

''I don't want the attention now!''

A small muscle pulled in his jaw. ''Strangely, darling, your behavior leads me to believe otherwise. Your color is high. Your breathing quick, your lovely lips parted. Truthfully you appear…exhilarated.''

Truthfully she felt overwrought. She was torn between excitement and anger, her skin acutely sensitive to him, her nerves too taut. Just the press of his lips to her wrist sent shiver after shiver streaking down her spine. And now, just like every other time, his touch undid her, her mind going blank, her body throbbing to life.

Dragging her gaze up, her eyes met his. His eyes, amber and flecked with bits of pale gold, glowed. She imagined she could see the fire behind the gold, the passion simmering within. He'd taught her everything about making love, made her body an instrument of pleasure…hers and his. She blushed, heat scorching through her skin, heightening the color in her cheeks.

He kissed her wrist again, his lips lingering against the slender bones, before linking her fingers in his. "We'll marry," he said quietly. "We'll try again to make our marriage work. But first, I think we should discuss a few things, air grievances, wipe the slate clean. Let's start with you. Why did you leave me three years ago?"

Did they have to do this now? It had to be close to midnight, she was dead on her feet and wanted nothing more than to creep into bed. "Can this wait, Kahlil? I'm exhausted. I haven't slept well in days."

"We can't start a marriage with ghosts hanging over our heads."

"Perhaps then, we should take some time to explore this, but not so late at night after the most impossibly long couple of days, and not after your cousin has spent two hours bragging about his gambling debts!" She felt her cheeks burn, her temper close to erupting. "Why do you tolerate him away? He's a leech, Kahlil, he doesn't even work."

Kahlil's jaw tightened, a small muscle popping close

to his ear. "He lives off his trust fund. It's his fund, his choice."

"You set up the trust fund. Not your father. That was your doing."

"And if it was?"

She missed the raspy pitch, his deepening inflection, too caught up in her own emotions to read Kahlil properly. Because if she had heard the caustic note in Kahlil's voice, she would have immediately known she was entering very dangerous territory.

"Kahlil, I understand the blood is thicker than water part, but he's not good for you. He's not loyal—"

"He'd said you'd say this. He bet me a thousand sterling pounds that you'd attack his loyalty, and his integrity. I owe him."

Bryn swallowed hard. "When did he say this?"

"Earlier. In my office. Before I went to change for dinner."

So Amin had approached Kahlil privately, rushing to reach him when she wasn't around. What a snake, what a cruel, poisonous snake. "He's a liar, Kahlil."

Kahlil sat forward, weight resting on his elbows, robe parting at the chest, displaying the bronzed plane of muscle. "Tell me, did anything happen between you two? Anything unflattering…anything possibly incriminating?"

She felt chilled to the bone. My God, *what* had Amin told Kahlil? "No! No. I can't stand him. He makes my skin crawl."

"Two lies, Bryn, two lies tonight. How can I possibly ever trust you?"

Bryn stood frozen, stunned. Her mouth worked, lips quivering, her brain struggling to sift through the truths and motivation. "I don't know what lies you're talking about."

"Lie number one—I asked you earlier if you had a problem with Amin and you said no. Lie number two—I asked you moments ago if something had happened between you and my cousin, and you said no." His eyes were riveted on her face, no mercy in his harsh expression. "Amin told me about your little…infatuation. It's been three years, enough time has passed, why can't we discuss it?"

She went to him, knelt before him, placed her hands on his knees. "Kahlil, I'll tell you why I don't like Amin. He destroys people, destroys the truth. I've never known anyone to twist the truth the way he does. I thought he was my friend but he's not. I confided in him, and spent time with him, but there was no sordid relationship."

"No kiss?"

"No. Never." She rose up higher on her knees, begging him to listen, to understand. "I wasn't attracted to him. I had you. But it made him angry. He wants to punish us—"

"Why would he do that?" Kahlil barked.

Gently she reached up, touched his jaw, pained by the way he flinched from her touch. Yet she didn't draw her hand away, she continued to caress his chin and the warmth of his mouth. ''Maybe because he envies our happiness.''

Kahlil caught her hand in his, holding it immobile. His gold eyes pierced her, searching for the truth. ''If he betrayed me, I want to know. If he took advantage of you, he will be punished. Is there something else I should be aware of?''

What was she to accuse Amin of? Assault? Rape? She'd sent him a note, asking him to meet her. It was essentially at her invitation that he came to her room. How could she explain Amin's threatening behaviour and still justify her own?

She couldn't.

''No,'' she said at length, sitting back slowly on her heels. ''There is nothing else.''

''I do not want you and Amin to be alone again. No more confidential talks. No more cups of tea or whatever you used to do. My wife must be above reproach. My wife must conduct herself in a manner befitting a princess. Understand?''

''Yes.''

''In one week we say our vows,'' Kahlil said slowly, enunciating clearly, ''and this time, no secrets, no lies. No runaway brides.''

The week passed with unusual swiftness. Bryn spent her days with Ben, nights with Kahlil, and saw virtually nothing of Amin. In fact, after going three days without a single glimpse of Kahlil's cousin, Bryn wondered if perhaps Amin had returned to Monte Carlo. She grinned, liking the thought. No more Amin, no more of his threats, no more worrying about his twisted intentions.

Amin, however, only got passing attention. Kahlil dominated her thoughts. It was almost as if he was superimposing himself on her life. He had moved her permanently into his room at night, located Ben's nursery in a nearby suite and took most meals with Bryn, and whenever possible, with his son also.

At night Kahlil loved to undress her, seduce her, savor her. He made love so thoroughly that when she finally slept, she drifted off into deep, dreamless slumber. Sometimes he'd wake her in the night to claim her again, but always by morning, he'd be gone, dressed, in his office, conducting business and meetings.

She overheard Kahlil on the phone once. It seemed he was required to participate in a conference, but Kahlil was giving his apologies, explaining he couldn't go, that leaving Tiva wasn't an option at the moment.

He wouldn't leave her alone, she realized, more unsettled than reassured. He didn't trust her.

She tried asking him about the conference over dinner, attempting to give him reassurance that things would be fine in the palace if he needed to attend. Kahlil nearly snapped her head off. "I will not leave you here alone."

His voice echoed, his tone razor-sharp. "But I wouldn't be alone," she answered mildly. "Rifaat, Lalia, the castle guards, Ben."

"I'm not going. End of discussion."

He didn't touch her that night in bed, and Bryn fell

asleep, huddled in a little ball, feeling like a stranger sleeping in Kahlil's bed but not part of his heart.

Would things never be the same between them again?

The next time he reached for her, he made love with an intensity that left her breathless and dizzy. It was as if he was reclaiming her, branding her, reminding her of possession. She was his. She belonged to him. But he didn't, wouldn't, love her.

The morning of the wedding arrived. In her old suite of rooms, Lalia attended Bryn, drawing a bath, then drying her with scrupulous care before applying a perfumed oil to her skin.

Lalia sang as she helped Bryn dress, her dark eyes lit with excitement. "This is a happy day, yes? You marry the Sheikh al-Assad here, nice traditional ceremony, and everyone be very happy."

Except for Bryn. She wanted Kahlil to show her some sign of affection, some hint that he might have deeper emotions, but he kept everything hidden. Their conversations were banal. The only time they were close was at night in his bed. Otherwise they were practically strangers, distant and detached.

A knock sounded on the door and Lalia went to answer it. She returned with a folded sheet of paper.

Bryn stared at the scrap of paper, darts of anxiety pricking her spine. Only one person had ever passed notes in the palace. Only one person would dare send her a note in the women's quarters.

Slowly she unfolded the sheet of paper. *I must see*

*you. Immediately.* No name, but she didn't need one. She knew the handwriting. Amin.

For a second she couldn't breathe and then, when feeling returned, she fiercely squeezed her hand closed, crumpling the note. She wouldn't answer him. He didn't deserve an answer. He shouldn't even be here. What was he doing in the palace on her wedding day? Shouldn't he be back in Monte Carlo, gambling and partying?

Bryn was tempted to send for Kahlil, to confess everything once and for all. Better face the music, get the whole episode with Amin put behind them before they renewed their vows. But she hesitated, feeling the wadded note in the palm of her hand.

Would Kahlil understand if she told him? Would he realize why she'd allowed herself to trust a man like Amin?

No. Kahlil needed no one. He didn't like weakness in others. He despised it in himself. No matter what she said about Amin, the fact was that he and Kahlil were once inseparable, practically brothers.

Amin had her backed into a corner and he knew it. But she wouldn't give in, and she wouldn't give up. This was her home now, her family. Perhaps she couldn't speak against Amin, but she didn't have to play his game, either.

The wedding gown was a pale shade of gold encrusted with precious jewels. It clung elegantly to her slender frame, catching the light as she moved beneath crystal chandeliers and passed ornate wall mirrors. The wedding party was waiting for her outside. Lalia led the way, brimming with excitement. Suddenly a hand clamped around her upper arm and dragged her to a step. "What is that American expression? 'You can run, but you can't hide?'"

Bryn watched Lalia continue walking. Her heart raced uncomfortably fast. "You've watched too many movies, Amin. Let go of me."

"We need to talk."

"There's nothing to discuss." But he ignored her, forcibly dragging her down the hall to a discreet door tucked between oversize gilt mirrors.

Amin pulled her into a broom closet and shut the narrow door behind them. "I can make your life hell, if that's what I choose."

"You only think you can." She bristled, furious that he'd try something like this minutes before the ceremony. She wasn't afraid. More irritated than anything. Why didn't Kahlil realize Amin was an underhanded sneak? How could Kahlil tolerate such a person in his life? "You're a fake, and a phony, and if you continue to make threats I will tell Kahlil *everything* about you."

"Don't push me, Miss America."

"And don't you push me! I'm not the naïve bride of five years ago, and I've had more than enough of your sordid little games. You attacked me that night in my room, you were going to rape me—"

He caught her by the upper arm, his fingers digging hard into her flesh, hurting her. "You wanted it. You wanted *me*."

"Want you? I despise you! And if you don't let go I will scream bloody murder."

She reached for the doorknob but he stopped her, pressing himself against the length of her, his hand covering her mouth, another arm around her throat. "I wouldn't scream, and I wouldn't go to Kahlil if I were you because he won't understand. He's a sheikh, an Eastern man with Eastern thinking. He won't forgive a wife that's betrayed him. He won't forgive you. Ever."

Bryn bit his fingers and swung out from beneath his arm. "Stay away from me!" she cried, flinging the door open.

Her legs shook as she walked down the hall toward the open doorway where everyone was gathered. She saw the clustered servants but couldn't think clearly, thoughts tangled, emotions wild, tears pricking her eyes. Amin muddled truth and lies better than anyone she knew.

He also knew her fears, which gave him a horrible amount of power over her. He knew she was afraid of being abandoned. Knew she was terrified of being thrown out and separated from her beloved Ben.

With a trembling hand she smoothed her wrinkled shirt and adjusted her headpiece. Her heart continued to pump wildly and she couldn't silence Amin's voice, his words echoing around and around in her head. *Kahlil's a sheikh, he's Eastern and his thinking is Eastern...*

Bryn silently cursed herself, hating that she'd ever shared so much of her feelings with Amin. Amin knew she used to be insecure. He knew she probably still fought that same insecurity now. It didn't take much to topple one's confidence. The right words, the right accusations, the right seeds planted...

*"No!"* She wouldn't—couldn't—let Amin do this to them again. He'd come between her and Kahlil once before and he'd destroyed their marriage, but she refused to allow it to happen again. She was stronger this time. More confident. She knew what she wanted and it was Kahlil.

This was her wedding day. She wasn't about to let anyone—much less Amin—ruin it.

Outside sunshine poured across the smooth tiles and Bryn drew a deep breath, calmer, more focused. Quiet laughter and eager voices surged around her. Everyone was excited about the festivities. She was excited. This was the start to a brand-new life for her and Ben, a brand-new future.

Rifaat and Lalia were waiting for her just outside the door. "Was there a problem?" Rifaat asked, his gaze moving past her, searching the long dark hall.

Bryn forced a smile to her lips, her body still cold but the trembling less obvious. "Everything's fine."

Rifaat's brows knotted, dark slashes above gray eyes. "I thought I saw his highness' cousin—"

"Yes, you did. I passed Amin in the hall. He was just heading to his room."

Rifaat's gaze swept the hall once more before turning to her, surveying her pale composed face. She saw his eyes focus on her neck. His eyebrows flattened. Self-consciously she reached up, touched the spot where he was staring. The skin felt tender. Amin might have bruised her. Her stomach flip-flopped and yet she couldn't do anything about it now. This was a happy day, a day she'd waited years for. She wasn't going to let Amin spoil another moment. "Are we ready?" she asked.

"Yes, Princess," Lalia answered, reaching up to cover Bryn's mouth and nose with the filmy scrap of fabric. "Time to go. His highness is waiting."

She joined Kahlil at the palace gate, butterflies replacing her fear, anticipation making her warm, almost too eager. She felt like a real bride—felt jittery and anxious, happy and a little tearful. To become Kahlil's wife in Kahlil's country. To marry in his sacred ceremony. To exchange vows in his language.

It felt right. Felt perfect. But her idea of perfection disappeared when Kahlil stepped aside and she caught a whiff of her least favorite mode of transportation. "A camel, Kahlil?"

Faint creases fanned from the corners of his eyes as he took her hand in his and kissed her fingers. "It's custom."

She balked beneath the ornate arch festooned with boughs of flowers. "You know how I feel about camels."

"You had one bad experience, *laeela*. This one hasn't bitten anyone in months."

She glared at Kahlil, giving him the full weight of her disapproval. They were newlyweds when they'd taken that last camel ride. Kahlil's camel behaved beautifully.

Hers dumped her. Flat on her backside and then had the gall to take a bite.

And from Kahlil's expression she could see he remembered, too. He'd picked the camels on purpose. It was his way of linking her—today—to the past. "As long as he doesn't spit, too. I don't want to ruin my hair. Lalia spent two and a half hours making it look like this."

"On my honor, I won't let this one spit."

Her lips twitched. "You can do something about prices of oil, Sheikh al-Assad, but even you can't control a camel."

And yet, looking at him now, seeing him dressed in the traditional wedding *djellaba,* the *howli* on his head, he never looked more fierce, more Arabic, and more sensual than now. Truthfully, she would have ridden beneath the camel's belly if he'd asked her.

But he didn't ask her, thank goodness. He smiled at her, his golden gaze locking with hers. "You look beautiful, have I told you that yet?"

Blood rushed to her cheeks, making her skin hot and tingly. "No."

"I've never met a more beautiful woman in my life. I'm honored you've consented to be my wife."

She couldn't speak for a moment, couldn't even swallow, her heart thudding hard, her chest tender with love. She'd never loved any other man the way she loved him. He made her feel real—complete. "I want to make you happy," she whispered, not trusting her voice.

"You have."

And for a split second they were the only two alive, the only two breathing, thinking, feeling. She felt the world wrap around them, snug, vivid, perfect. If only it could always be this way.

"Come," he said, taking her hand, "your camel awaits. And so does our son. My cousin Mala has flown in from London with her children. She's taken Ben to the ceremony with them and they're waiting, impatiently, I imagine."

Once seated on the kneeling camel, house servants crowded behind, filling the courtyard. Lalia rushed forward to adjust Bryn's elaborate gown. The servants cheered as Kahlil took his camel and the cheer turned into music once his camel arose. With flower petals cascading, and the hauntingly evocative music echoing, the camels set off. Bryn lifted her hand, waved to the crowd behind, and caught a tender pink petal in her hand. Her heart beat quickly. This time, she silently vowed, she and Kahlil would last forever.

# CHAPTER TEN

THE scene was just like a set from an old movie studio: enormous white tent, tethered camels, luxurious ruby-red Persian carpets lining the shady tent interior. Music and palms, enormous fronds swaying with the late-afternoon breeze. The sun was just setting, as Kahlil had predicted, painting the creamy dunes of sand red, peach, gold.

The ceremony, beautiful as it was, passed in a blur of prayers, blessings, and the joining of their hands. Then it was over and Kahlil was guiding her to the helicopter that had just touched down, Kahlil's hand in the small of her back, his warmth doing something crazy to her senses.

"Where are we going?" she asked, buckling her seat belt and glancing out the open door to catch a glimpse of Ben. Kahlil had already told her that Ben would be staying at the palace while they were gone, taken care of by the palace nanny and Kahlil's cousin Mala who had two little boys of her own. Ben was thrilled at the chance to play with other children and yet it was always hard for Bryn to leave him.

But Ben, catching her eye, grinned and waved and she waved back. At least he wasn't worried about her going away with Kahlil for a few days. He was so confident. So much like his father.

149

She looked at Kahlil and he met her gaze. ''We're going to a special place of mine,'' he said. ''A place you've never been before.''

''Is it far?'' she asked.

She caught the wry curve of his mouth, his expression was boyish, almost exultant. He looked as though the weight of the world had been pulled from his shoulders. ''Not unless one's traveling by camel.''

It was dark when the helicopter landed. The sky was the darkest of purple with pinpricks of light and the ground below was a deep shadow, no glow of street lamps, no hint of civilization.

In this shapeless, formless nowhere the helicopter began to descend, lowering straight down into a sea of black. This meant they were either landing in the middle of an ocean or a sea of sand.

Bryn heard the helicopter pilot speak, giving directions into his headset. She frowned as the helicopter lowered, then caught small points of light, shimmering light, like miniature flames. And as the helicopter touched ground, Bryn realized the shimmering light was actually flames, burning torches set in a large circle around the helicopter pad.

''Where are we?'' she whispered.

''My hideaway.'' He took her hand, and ducking beneath the still whirring blades, they ran through ancient stone arches into a very old fortress that had to date back at least a thousand years.

''This is yours?'' she said, still breathless from the dash into the palace. Kahlil had swung her into his arms at the last moment before entering a high-ceiling bed-chamber with silk pillows strewn across the floor and candles burning in rugged wall sconces. ''Ah, and more candles. Didn't realize you loved firelight so much.''

''No electricity,'' he answered, drawing her down on the low mattress. ''I don't have a choice. If we didn't have candles, I couldn't see you, and believe me, I want to see you.''

She felt heat creep into her cheeks, her limbs suddenly weak. ''You do?''

He reclined backward. ''Yes, very much so. I'm actually dying to get you naked.'' His voice lowered, turned husky. ''Strip for me.''

''Wh…what?''

''I want to watch you undress and then inspect my wife.''

She was shocked, and yet strangely aroused.

''You said you'd obey me,'' he quietly chided, reminding her of her promises. ''You said we'd have a real relationship.''

''Yes, but…''

His eyebrow cocked. He simply looked at her, waiting.

Blood flooding her cheeks, fingers trembling, she reached for the narrow zipper at the side of her gown. Kahlil leaned back on the bed, watching. With short, nervous tugs, she worked the zipper down and then carefully stepped out of the lavishly embroidered dress.

Next came the narrow silk straps of her bustier. She

pushed the satin fabric down, toward her waist, exposing her breasts.

"Ah."

Bryn swayed beneath the intense scrutiny, feeling Kahlil's heat and interest, aware of his gaze as he drank in her bared breasts, the pale skin taut, the pink nipples hard, aching, like the ache between the thighs.

"The rest, please."

He sounded completely indifferent but he wasn't; he was a study of concentration. Shyly she tugged her satin panties over her hips, to her knees, and pulled them from her ankles. Completely naked, except for the gold jewel-studded crown she still wore in her hair, she blushed, warm color rushing from her toes to her head.

Wordlessly Kahlil rose, drew her to him, pressing her naked length to his. He was hard everywhere, his chest, his abdomen, his thighs, but it was his erection that generated more heat in her, his own hunger throbbing at the V of her thighs.

His arms encircled her, his hands cupped her bare bottom, the curve of her derriere in each of his palms. He lifted her slightly, drawing her closer, pressing her against the thrust of his desire. Her inner thighs clenched. Her belly tightened. She felt empty inside, empty and deprived.

"You're so warm," he murmured in her ear, his voice rich, seductive. "You feel like heaven."

"I think it feels like hell," she protested, shiver after shiver racing through her, his chest brushing against her aching nipples, intensifying her sensitivity.

"You just need to learn patience."

"I'm trying." Bryn rose on her tip toes, slowly circling his neck with one arm, and then the other, drawing their bodies even closer. His chest crushed the bare fullness of her breasts. Her calves balled into hard knots of muscle and her abdomen stretched, long, lean.

"Lovely," he murmured, fingers caressing the curve of her spine, then rising to play each vertebrae in her back.

She liked it better with his hand in her lower back, his hard length tight against her mound, her body desperately drinking him in. Feverish, Bryn nipped his beard-roughened chin and then his mouth. "Kiss me back," she begged. "Kiss me like you used to."

In response he swung her into his arms and carried her to the bed covered in luxurious silks and satin. She smelled his signature fragrance of sandalwood and citrus and cupping his face in her hands, kissed him deeply even as she tugged at his robe.

There were no more formalities, no more foreplay. It wasn't long before both were swept away, carried to the highest peak of pleasure. And for the first time since returning to Zwar, she felt a wall come down between them, some invisible barrier breaking and Kahlil held her, kissed her, loved her with profound tenderness.

Warm tears pricked the back of her eyes but these were tears of hope. They would make this work. They would find happiness after all.

Shudders still coursing through her, Kahlil shifted Bryn in his arms, drawing her down to the mattress beside him. "You are mine, do you understand? Mine, all mine."

"Yes, master."

His eyes glinted, and smiling faintly he kissed the corner of her mouth, and then the soft full lower lip still throbbing with blood and passion. "I like the sound of that," he murmured.

"I know you do."

"Are you sure you're not just humoring me?"

"Could I be any more obedient?"

"That's different from a surrender." But he laughed, the sound rich, deep, husky. "And I'll just have to step up my training."

Still smiling, he kissed her again, his laughter warming her mouth, stealing her breath. She felt tingles rush through her, pleasure and happiness. If Kahlil was letting down his guard enough to laugh with her, she knew she'd found her way back into his heart. He might not tell her in words he loved her, but the tenderness was there, hidden within him. She'd just give him time. Lavish him with love. It was all they needed—time and love.

He kissed her neck, and the hollow beneath her ear. She felt heat explode inside her, her desire for his insatiable. "Don't start anything you're not prepared to finish," she softly teased, locking her hands behind his neck and drawing his mouth down to hers.

"Oh, I'm prepared," he answered, shifting his weight, settling between her thighs, and from all impressive evidence, he most certainly was. He nipped at her lip, teeth sharp, hunger barely restrained. "You do know I've cheated to get you back, don't you? I told a little lie—"

Bryn's hands flew to his shoulders and pushed him back. "What?"

"It's not a big deal. Practically a white lie."

White lie? Kahlil? "And just what was this *white lie?*"

He kissed her again, ignoring her attempts to evade his mouth, and finally she melted beneath him, resistance fading. He smiled against her lips, acknowledging her feeble defense. "Well, I did pay a certain official to destroy a certain piece of paper. That document you never signed? My fault. I made sure it never reached you."

"Kahlil!"

He clasped her face in his hands, kissed her fiercely. "I wasn't going to lose you. I never wanted to lose you."

Suddenly they were interrupted by a pounding on the bedroom door. "Go away," Kahlil shouted, smiling wickedly at Bryn, his hand moving across her belly to her thighs. "I'm busy."

"Forgive me, your highness," the voice answered from the far side of the door. "But this is an emergency."

Kahlil was gone less than five minutes. "A problem has come up in Tiva," he said, returning to the bedchamber and flinging a shirt over his shoulders. "It's urgent. I must return to the palace immediately."

He was dressing in Western clothes. His brow furrowed deeply, his expression was nothing but grim. "I'll be back as soon as I can."

Something in his expression unnerved her. Bryn sat up in bed. "What kind of problem?"

"Can't discuss it just yet. But I'll send the helicopter for you first chance I get."

"You're going to leave me here, in the middle of nowhere?"

"It's safe. It's my home. I want you here."

It was a no-argument tone, one of his submit-and-surrender expressions.

"At least tell me what you do know."

"Bryn, I wish I could. I don't have all the facts."

"But something at the palace?" Immediately her thoughts turned to Ben. He was there. He was there without her. "Has there been an uprising?"

"No, nothing like that."

"Then what? My God, Kahlil, the baby—"

"*I know.*" He clasped her hard by the shoulders, kissed her forehead, his mouth a brief imprint of heat against her skin. "Be patient. I'll learn more soon."

He released her, grabbed an overcoat and swung toward the door.

Sixteen hours later Kahlil reappeared. He'd only just returned to the crumbling fortress. Bryn could still hear the rotary whir of the helicopter blades.

"It's Ben," Kahlil said sharply, without preamble. His complexion looked ashen, deep purple shadows beneath his bloodshot eyes. "He's gone."

Ben. Gone. Impossible. But that's what Kahlil had said.

Through a narrow window Bryn saw clouds of red-gold spiral, desert sand swirling furiously. Her mind was like that, swirling, dizzying. "What do you mean gone? Gone where?"

"We don't know."

*You don't know?* An irrational voice screamed inside her head. *You're the sheikh. The king. You must know.* She wrapped her arms across her chest, lifted her chin, fighting for calm. "Did he run away?"

"No."

"Then what? Are you telling me someone *kidnapped* Ben?"

"Yes."

She staggered backward, eyes widening. Her mouth felt dry, her tongue like lead. Disbelief surged through her veins. "Who?" Her voice came out a whisper, airless, powerless, a flutter of sound.

"Amin."

She took another half step backward and Kahlil's shoulders shifted, an uneasy gesture that revealed more than his words could. "I have every resource working on this, Bryn. We will find them. That's a promise."

She felt as though she'd plunged into an icy river and her body was shutting down, legs numb, muscles numb, heart freezing.

This was her fault.

She hadn't protected Ben, hadn't confided her fears in Kahlil. She'd felt strong, impervious to Amin. She'd even challenged him, taunted him that he couldn't hurt her, that he wasn't powerful enough. My God. What had she done?

Helplessly she crunched her fingers to her palms, folded her arms against her breasts, fighting to stay warm. She felt cold, desperately cold, and desperately afraid. "What do you know right now? What are your leads?"

"Ben was taken last night after the ceremony. The maid was drawing his bath, had her back turned while filling the tub. When she went to fetch Ben, he was gone."

Gone. The word conjured terror. Puff, gone. Puff, lost. Puff, her heart broken.

She pressed the tip of her tongue to the roof of her mouth but her mind went blank. What could she say? Nothing. Nothing. Finally, after long, impenetrable seconds, she stuttered, "How do you know Amin took him? How do you know he didn't wander off? That he didn't get out through an open door?"

"We have evidence."

"What evidence?" She refused to be thwarted. This wasn't a lost set of car keys, for God's sake, but their *child!*

"Amin left a note." Deep grooves formed on either side of Kahlil's mouth. "It was cryptic. Didn't really make sense. We just need to be patient and let my men continue their investigation."

If he'd hoped to calm her, he'd failed. His words only

incited greater alarm. Her stomach heaved. "Tell me, Kahlil. I want to know. I *need* to know."

"The note was short. And as I've said, cryptic. Amin wrote that he was taking what was his. That's all he said."

Relief washed over her. "So we don't know that Amin has Ben. We have two missing people. We don't know they're together."

"But we do." Kahlil's lips compressed, the lines near his mouth almost white. "We have it on videotape, Amin bundling Ben up and carrying him from the nursery."

"No! Not like that, he didn't do that, tell me, Kahlil—"

Kahlil caught Bryn in his arms and drew her close, cradling her against her chest. "Shh, *laeela,* we'll find them. We'll have our son home soon. I swear."

The helicopter returned them to Tiva, landing in the gated palace courtyard. The whirring blades blew the palms, creating a swish of green against the white plaster walls.

A scarlet-throat hummingbird buzzed past their heads, flitting to one of the pots of coral-red hibiscus flanking the door. Bryn paused for a split second to watch the emerald-green bird dive into the petals. That is how she'd been with Kahlil, the hummingbird unable to resist the nectar.

And look what her desire, her intense love, had done to them. Secrets, lies, a kidnapped baby.

It was almost too much to bear.

Kahlil gently touched her spine, prompting Bryn through the enormous door. He walked her to her suite of rooms, stopping outside the harem entrance. With a kiss on her upturned lips, he promised, "I'll send word as soon as I hear something."

He felt warm and solid, and she found comfort in his proximity. It was easier facing the future with Kahlil at her side. "I don't want to be alone," she pleaded, fingers grappling, tangling in his robe. "Let me stay with you."

"This is a high-level security matter. I'll be meeting with my advisors. It's better if you stay here."

"It's not better for me. I'm scared."

"Bryn, trust me." He plucked her hands from his robe, gave her an encouraging smile, although the deep lines fanning from his eyes told another story. "I promise I'll let you know as developments occur. Now try to rest. You need it."

Lalia ordered a small dinner tray that Bryn didn't touch. She didn't want food. She wanted Ben home.

Minutes turned to hours. The wait grew intolerable. Two hours. Three. Her back ached, her head hurt. Her eyes felt like small rough pebbles, too dry from so little sleep.

Four hours passed. Bryn began to shake, the after shocks of adrenaline. Too little sleep. Too much anxiety. She felt as if she were turned inside out and about to break.

"You must sleep, my lady," Lalia soothed, drawing down the cool sheets, dimming the bedside lamp. "Lie down. Rest."

But Bryn couldn't sleep, and she spent the night sitting against the wall of her bedroom, her gaze fixed on the distant horizon.

Amin was evil, the worst kind of evil, but not even he would actually hurt Ben, would he?

She tried to imagine where Amin had taken Ben, wondering if it was very dark, and if Ben was frightened. But her mind shied away from a morbid scenario. She had to remain positive, had to believe that Ben was fine and that Amin would be kind.

Comforted somewhat, Bryn watched the moon shift in the sky, arcing slowly through the night, the stars growing whiter, brighter, only to dim again, until at last the purple faded to violet and then to lavender.

The morning sun rose and Bryn still sat, her back against the wall, her arms encircling her knees.

The maid reappeared, shrouded in filmy veils. She, too, looked tired, as though she hadn't slept. ''Breakfast, Princess,'' she said, delivering a tray with sweet breads, fresh fruit and hot mint tea.

''I can't eat. Not until Ben's home.''

''The sheikh will bring him home. The sheikh is all-powerful.''

All-powerful. If only it were true! Bryn sipped her tea but didn't touch the food, staring at the sliced mango on the tray, the fruit's vivid flesh ripe and juicy. She wondered what Ben would have for breakfast. She prayed Amin would give him breakfast. If Ben were even still alive… No! You can't think like that. Of course he's alive. Amin is cruel and selfish, but he wouldn't hurt a child.

Tears filled her eyes and she bit her knuckles, determined not to cry, not to give in to useless emotion. Tears wouldn't help Ben.

A rustle of fabric, Lalia in the doorway. Her features were drawn. "My lady, Sheikh al-Assad is waiting in the main reception room. Please, I dress you quickly.'

Bryn fidgeted as Lalia dressed her in a simple apricot chiffon gown. "You must be brave, Princess," Lalia urged, combing Bryn's hair smooth and tying it with an apricot ribbon.

"I am very brave," Bryn answered grimly. She wanted nothing so much as to be with Kahlil and to discover his news. She could only pray that he'd located Ben.

Rifaat waited for her at the entrance to the women's quarters. "Good morning, Princess al-Assad."

Bryn had grown so accustomed to his silence that his greeting startled her. "Good morning, Rifaat."

"You look very tired. Are you not sleeping?"

How could she? How could anyone sleep when a three-year-old was missing? "Has his highness heard anything?"

"That I do not know."

Her eyebrows arched, impatience, frustration balling into one. "Why must we play these games, Rifaat? You know everything that happens in this place. You're Kahlil's secret ears. You're privy to all the servants' gossip. You often know things before Kahlil!"

Rifaat almost smiled, but the expression in his deep brown eyes was infinitely sad. ''A blessing, and a curse, my lady. Sometimes it is better not to know.'' And with another slight bow he led the way through the gleaming marble hall, past the center pavilion and down another breezeway.

Bryn immediately spotted Kahlil at the far end of the reception room. He stood at an open window overlooking the private patio. Soft gold light washed the windowsill, the sky still the fairy-tale pink of early morning.

Kahlil was the only one in the room. He slowly turned from the window and moved to a massive chair with burgundy cushions and sat down even more slowly.

He didn't make eye contact. He didn't even look at her.

Bryn's stomach dropped. This was bad. Very, very bad. Something terrible had happened to Ben.

# CHAPTER ELEVEN

"TELL me," she whispered. "Tell me what's happened."

"Come closer."

She was frozen, petrified of what he might say. "Tell me first. Just get it over with."

His dark head lifted, his eyes, brilliant with emotion, met hers. "I've heard nothing about Ben. This has to do with you."

She shuffled forward, one step, and then another, adrenaline still surging, too much tension and exhaustion for her to think clearly. "Me?"

"Yes, my dutiful wife, you."

"What have you heard? What's this about?"

"What have you heard?" He repeated her words, enunciating the consonants as though they were sharp things in his mouth. "Oh, I've learned quite a bit, read quite a bit, too."

"I don't understand."

"You bluff, Princess." He rose from his chair and descended the dais. His feet were bare, his robe open, revealing long white trousers and the bronze of his chest. "Sit down."

She sank to the cushion in front of her, a burgundy

silk embroidered with gold thread. "You've totally confused me. I have no idea what you're talking about."

"None?"

She leaned away from Kahlil as he marched a circle around her, scowling, his hands knotted behind his back. He wasn't making sense. She'd been nowhere, gone nowhere. How could she have displeased him? "What does any of this have to do with *Ben?*"

"The correct question should be, what does any of this have to do with *Amin?*"

The sinking feeling returned. Kahlil had obviously heard something, learned something. Had Amin made a threat? Told stories? How had he incriminated her now?

"Well?" Kahlil stopped in front of her, rocked back on his heels. "You're not going to defend yourself?"

Beads of perspiration formed across her forehead and on her nape. "I can't defend myself if I do not know the charge."

"I want to know about your affair with Amin."

Her skin felt clammy and cold despite the warm morning and the moisture on her brow. "There was no affair."

"That's not what the videotape shows."

"There is no videotape of Amin and I together—"

"There is plenty of video tape of you two together."

"But not of us having sex."

"Tell me, was he, or was he not in your room?"

Dear God, how did he know that? It must have been Amin. Amin must have confessed. "He was, but nothing like that happened."

"Yet you ran away. Perhaps because you felt guilty?"

She couldn't believe he'd do this now, when Ben was missing. "We had no affair. We never had sex. Look at your videotape for proof!"

"There's no surveillance camera in the harem. The camera stops at the door."

"How convenient!"

"But this wasn't a one-night stand. You have been passing love letters for months."

"They weren't love letters, they were notes, very childish notes—"

"I don't think they're all that childish," he ground out, drawing slips of paper from a pocket in his robe. *"Amin, you've been too wonderful. I don't know what I'd do without you."* He unfolded another. *"I must see you tonight. When can we meet?* Or, how about this one? *You're an angel. I adore you."* Kahlil's dark head lifted. "I adore you? What the hell does that mean?"

"It means nothing, it meant nothing. They were schoolgirl notes. I was eighteen!"

"And married to me."

"I know it looks bad—"

"Looks bad? It *is* bad. What the hell were you doing writing love letters?"

"They weren't love letters, they were messages between friends. Amin was giving me advice—"

"I bet he was."

She flinched at the snarl in his voice. "It's not like that, Kahlil. Please try to understand. We'd returned to Zwar and you immediately buried yourself in work. I was lonely, overwhelmed, I felt totally out of my element.''

"So you turned to Amin."

"For friendship, and friendship only. He once was very kind to me. He listened to me, encouraged me, made me believe that everything would soon be better between you and me."

"So I'm at fault? I was a lousy husband?"

"No, Kahlil, please try to understand. When we were dating you were so attentive, you made me feel special, and very loved. Maybe I was spoiled—"

"Maybe?"

"All right, I was spoiled, and immature, but the fact is when we returned here, you buried yourself in work and you had so little time for me. Amin befriended me. He realized I was lonely, lacking confidence, and he made me believe everything would be okay."

"You don't tell another man you are lonely and lacking confidence. You tell me. You don't turn to another man for comfort, you turn to me."

The savagery in his voice ripped through her. His features contorted, a dark violence in his expression, a bitterness she'd never seen before.

"Kahlil, please forgive me. I beg you."

"Spare me the apology, Bryn, it's a little late for that, don't you think?"

"I never meant to hurt you. I love you. I've always loved you."

He made a rude sound. "Amin says Ben is his." His voice whipped her again. "If that's so, Amin has every right to take the boy. I have no legal or moral reason to recover him for you.''

"No!''

"The search has been called off.''

She nearly screamed in protest. Hands outstretched. "My God, Kahlil, you can't mean it. Ben's a baby. He must be terrified.''

"Amin can handle it.''

"Amin isn't Ben's father. *You are.* And I've never been with another man, so even if you're angry, don't punish Ben. He doesn't even know Amin!''

"It's not my problem anymore.''

"Not your problem? You're the sheikh of Zwar. Your cousin has kidnapped your child. You say it's not your problem? Who runs this bloody country anyway?''

Kahlil grabbed her wrist and swung her against his chest, slamming the air from her lungs. "Do you know who you're speaking to?''

"My husband!'' Tears rushed to her eyes. "My arrogant, prideful pigheaded husband. You know why I turned to Amin all those years ago? Because you shut me out. You stopped seeing me, hearing me, talking to me. I was lonely and I wasn't very good at being lonely, but I never slept with Amin and if you dare risk your child's safety out of pride—'' she drew a deep, staggering breath ''—I swear, Kahlil, I'll…''

"What will you do?''

"I'll search for them myself. I won't eat, sleep, rest until I find them.''

"You're a woman in the Middle East. You have no

money, no transportation, no friends. You'll never find them.''

Her heart was breaking. ''Why do you hate me so much? Is it because I'm weak? Because I have needs?''

''Your needs drove you into my brother's arms.'' He released her swiftly, his scathing tone blistering, drawing blood to her cheeks. ''You make me sick.''

She didn't hear the last part, just the first part and it echoed in her head. His brother? ''You mean *cousin's* arms.''

''Amin is my brother.'' He swallowed, his jaw thickening. ''My half brother. My mother's bastard son.''

Stunned, Bryn held her breath. She felt the blackness of Kahlil's mood, his confession wrung in pain and anger. ''I thought your mother died after you were born.''

''She didn't die. Not until I was in high school. When my father discovered her affair with his best friend, he exiled her from Zwar.'' His lashes lowered, accenting the harsh sweep of his prominent cheekbones. ''My father was kind. Under our law, she could have been killed.''

''If your father was truly kind, he wouldn't have deprived you of your mother!''

''My mother chose to betray the marriage vow. She paid the consequence.''

''No, *you* paid the consequence! She made a mistake and you suffered for it. Just like you want Ben to suffer for my mistake, but that's not fair.''

''Life isn't fair, Bryn. It's never been fair. Ben might as well learn that now.''

"You can't mean that."

"I do. Life's full of hard knocks. I was lonely as a child. I suffered, too, but I'm here, stronger for it."

"Knowing that you suffered, remembering the pain, you'd inflict that on your own son?"

"I don't even know that he is my son."

"Yes, you do. He's you, he's yours. You might be angry with me, but you can't deny your own child."

"Did you sleep with him, Bryn?"

He'd changed the conversation, switched the focus in a split second, but she followed the leap, and her emotions swung from rage to pity to helplessness. "No, Kahlil, *no*. I'm not attracted to Amin. I've never been attracted to Amin."

"But these notes, his visit to your room, they clearly show that there was more than a friendship between you."

"Not on my part. I never wanted him, never imagined more. I can see how the notes could be misinterpreted, and I realize now how immature I sounded, but truly, Kahlil, there was no affair, no desire, no physical relationship."

His lashes lifted again, revealing the brittle glitter in the golden depths. "Just an emotional one."

He wasn't going to go, wasn't going to help with the rescue, but when word came that Amin had been located, Kahlil didn't even hesitate. He might be furious with Bryn, but he'd never make the boy suffer. Without changing clothes, he dashed to the waiting limousine, settling into the back seat although his hands itched to take the steering wheel himself. He still couldn't fathom how Amin could take a child—not just his child, but *any* child. How could a man stoop so low?

As the limousine sped through the city Kahlil rubbed his temple, fingers massaging, but the tension didn't lift. It was time peace was restored to the palace. And time to exert some order. It had been so long since Kahlil felt in control. So long since he felt easy in his own home.

Bryn was going to have to go.

Kahlil closed his eyes and gritted his jaw against the livid thrust of pain. He barely felt the car jolt as it hit a deep pothole in the road, his emotions running hot and wild, a black violence he fought desperately to suppress.

He loved her. No doubt about it. He'd once worshiped her, too, but that was before she shattered his trust, never mind his heart.

For long moments he saw nothing, heard nothing, felt nothing but a raging grief—half anger, half sorrow—the same irrational emotion a young child would feel. Knuckles pressed to squeezed eyelids he forced the scalding tears back. No crying over spilt milk. He couldn't change what had happened, and life moved on.

Move on.

*Move on, Kahlil, move on for God's sake.*

Long minutes later he dropped his hands, and gazed blankly out the limousine window. White bleached dunes swirled up around the sides of the road. Finally he could draw a breath without wanting to scream. He'd been through worse pain before; he'd survive losing

Bryn. He'd survive losing all of them. He was Sheikh Kahlil al-Assad and his word was law.

In the palace Lalia was doing her best to calm the princess, wringing out a damp scented cloth and placing it on Bryn's forehead. "Shh, my lady, you mustn't cry like that. You'll make yourself sick."

Bryn turned her head away, knocking off the cloth Lalia had pressed to her forehead. She didn't want a cool, damp cloth, mint tea, or conversation. She just wanted Kahlil, and Ben. She just wanted her family together again.

Bryn awoke with a start. Voices outside were shouting and an engine roared close to the palace entrance.

She'd fallen asleep while the sun was still bright, but now her bedroom was bathed in the lavender of twilight, the interior space violet, gray and cool.

Even as she sleepily stumbled to her feet, her bedroom door burst open. Dirty, bloodied, Kahlil marched toward the bed.

"Get up," he demanded. "We'll have this out. Once and for all."

A scarlet slash marred his forehead and his jaw was swollen. Another gash streaked his cheekbone. "You're hurt!"

He ignored her concern. "We have Ben, he appears fine, but I'm having my doctor see to him anyway. You will join him shortly."

"Thank God." She flung herself at Kahlil, wrapped her arms around his waist and held tight. "I knew you wouldn't leave him like that. I knew you'd find him."

He stood stiffly. ''I did it for him, not for you.''

She felt his rigid muscles, the tightening of his limbs. He was grinding his teeth, enduring the embrace. She could feel his anger and apathy, and his revulsion terrified her. What if he'd never forgive her? What if he couldn't forgive her? How would she live without him? ''Kahlil, I love you. I have always loved you and—''

He dragged her arms from him and pushed her away. ''I don't want to hear this.''

''But you must—''

''*No*. It's too late. Too late for any of this.'' With a hoarse sound, he pushed her away once again, holding himself stiffly. ''Amin waits for us. Let us get this over with.''

It was madness, what Kahlil was asking of her. Did he want her to confess to adultery, betrayal, to crimes she hadn't committed? Bryn refused to confess to anything other than failing to trust Kahlil when she was a new bride, but the rest she refuted verbally, and physically, with adamant shakes of her head.

Not Amin. He talked, or more accurately, smirked and talked, indicting her in his twisted fantasy. He insisted on clinging to his outrageous story, enlarging on it as the evening passed. He called her hot, passionate, insatiable.

Bryn shuddered as Amin elaborated, his lies making her skin crawl, his remembrances destroying her innocence, making her trust in him appear sordid.

Kahlil didn't look at Bryn as Amin talked. He stood before his ornate chair, arms crossed, expression blank.

And Bryn, knowing how his mother had failed him, knowing how he'd never felt secure in his father's love, realized she, too, had failed him. If Kahlil had wanted to torture her, he couldn't have picked a better punishment.

She saw Rifaat from the corner of her eye and the man stared off into space, silent, invisible. She shuddered, wondering what he must be thinking, what he must feel for a disloyal bride.

She'd failed them all.

Next time she'd do it differently. Next time she'd be stronger, tougher, braver. Next time she'd speak her mind early and ask the right questions and not hang on to grudges. Next time she'd be quick to forgive and even quicker to forget. Next time...

She closed her eyes, trying to keep the tears from falling but they gathered on her lashes and trembled there, against the curve of her cheek.

*Kahlil. I love you, Kahlil. Forgive me, Kahlil. You are my sun and my moon and everything...*

Kahlil's fingers snapped, loudly, too sharply. She opened her eyes to spot Kahlil marching toward Amin. "Enough, I've heard more than enough. The police are waiting outside, and somehow I think prison won't be as comfortable as your apartment in Monte Carlo."

"As if you ever cared," Amin snarled.

"I cared. You are my brother. You are my blood."

His mouth worked, his Adam's apple bobbed. "Blood? Since when? I've been nothing but your obligation, your charity case."

"I've shared with you everything."

Bryn shuddered at the rawness in Kahlil's voice. He sounded utterly bewildered.

"You shared with me nothing. You took my mother—"

"I lost her, too!" Kahlil interrupted hoarsely. "When my father sent her from Zwar, it broke me, too."

"But you recovered, crown prince of Zwar, you had all the opportunities, every advantage. Boarding schools in England. Graduate school in the U.S. Money, power. You had it all. I just wanted my share."

"My wife wasn't an option."

Suddenly Amin laughed, a high, hysterical pitch. "Wasn't she?"

Bryn covered her face with her hands. She couldn't bear it. She could hear the guards drag Amin from the room but didn't watch, didn't even look up until the heavy doors banged shut. But Amin wasn't the only one gone. Kahlil had left, too.

Bryn sat still for an agonizing moment, nervously rubbing the silky skirt of her gown. Rifaat remained in the room but he didn't speak to her. Finally, unable to bear the silence another moment, she blurted, "When is he coming back?"

Rifaat didn't immediately reply. She turned, glanced at him, noted his peculiar expression. "He is coming back, isn't he?"

"No, my lady."

She wasn't sure she'd heard correct. She bent her head. "But later, he'll send for me."

"I am to take you to your car. It's out front, waiting."

"And…Ben?"

"He's already in the car. With your things. Your servant has packed everything."

Bryn didn't understand, felt stupid for not understanding but it was all the excitement and the late hour and the fear of losing her baby. Now if only Rifaat would speak more slowly, explain it all again. "Why is Ben in the car? Where are we going?"

"Home."

But this was home. Kahlil and Bryn and the baby. This was where they belonged. So why was Ben in the car by himself? What was Kahlil doing putting Ben in the car by himself? How could Kahlil do that, how could he be so cruel? She jumped to her feet, her throat threatening to seal closed. "Where is Kahlil?"

"I know this is difficult, Princess, but perhaps his highness is correct. It would be wise to make a clean break. I am sure the crown prince is probably asleep in the limousine, and once you're on the plane, you will sleep, too. Soon this will just be a memory—"

"*No*. No, no, no." Kahlil couldn't do this. He had no right, not after dragging them here and putting them through hell. He'd awakened her heart, revived their love. He couldn't throw it back at her now! "I must see him."

"You can not, Princess—"

Bryn didn't wait to hear the rest, running from the royal chamber, racing down the long palace corridors, feet echoing against gleaming marble. She slipped past a pair of guards too startled to stop her, bursting into Kahlil's office suite but the rooms were dark, no one was there.

From a distance she heard Rifaat call her name but she ignored him, running on, racing toward Kahlil's bedroom. The door was shut. She tried the handle. It was locked and soft gold light poured from beneath the door.

''Kahlil!'' She cried his name, frantically pounding on the door, sensing Rifaat behind her. ''Listen to me. I understand you're angry, and you have every right. But don't punish the baby. Fight me, but not him! He loves you. He needs you. *I* need you.'' Her throat ached, her heart hurt, she shivered from head to toe. ''Dammit, Kahlil, how can we ever make this work if we won't ever talk to each other? Open the door, *please!*''

She wouldn't let Kahlil do this, couldn't let him shut her out again. She knew he loved her, deep down, somewhere in his hard, imperial heart. ''Oh, Kahlil, talk to me. You can't just put the baby and me on a plane and not say goodbye. What will we do without you? Where will we go? How can I raise Ben without you? If you're going to send me away at least give me some help— answers, advice, something Kahlil, please!''

Rifaat reached her, his hands closing on her shoulders as he attempted to pull her away from the sheikh's door. ''My lady, come, don't make me call the guards.''

Bryn broke free, pounding wildly against the door, desperation making her faint. ''Kahlil, help me.'' The door rattled beneath her pounding fist. ''They're going to take me away. You can stop them. You must stop them!''

Rifaat's hands settled again on her shoulders, gently this time, kindly. ''Please, Bryn,'' he spoke softly, urgently, using her name for the first time since she returned, ''you don't want to be carried out in disgrace. Go with dignity, I beg of you. For Ben's sake if nothing else.''

But she was fighting for Ben's sake, fighting for all their sakes. Kahlil needed them, just as much as she and Ben needed him. ''I will not go!'' she cried, pressing her forehead against the door, fingertips glued to the wood as if she could become one with the door and melt through. ''I will not.''

Rifaat applied more pressure to her shoulders, hands firm. ''I must see you to the car. Come with me, Bryn, don't make this harder than it already is.''

Salty tears raced down her cheek, streaking the door. ''Kahlil.'' She choked, breaking down, her vocal cords closing, shut down by her sobs.

The light beneath the door flickered casting a shadow on the other side. Hope returned, hope and anguish. ''In all my life, Kahlil, I've only loved you.''

Bryn could sense Kahlil on the other side of the door. She knew he must be there and she imagined she could feel his heart beat, feel his warmth and his sinewy strength. Closing her eyes she pressed her palm where she thought his chest must be. She needed to reach out to touch his heart. His anger pulsated through her palm. She felt his anger, his indecision and his pride. Before he could walk away, she knelt down and slid her fingers beneath the door, entreating, "I would walk to the ends of the earth for you. I would give up my heart if you demanded it. Kahlil " and suddenly his shadow receded. She felt him move away from her. Physically. Emotionally. He was shutting her out. Moving on. *Kahlil!*

Rifaat and a guard hauled her to her feet. She didn't have the strength to resist, all air sucked from her lungs in numb disbelief.

It was over. Kahlil didn't want her. Kahlil didn't want Ben. He'd made the decision and he wasn't going to change his mind.

Outside the driver waited in the limousine, behind the steering wheel. The back door to the black limousine stood open and Bryn spotted Ben, curled up on the back seat, beneath a soft blanket, sound asleep, his small arm clutching a stuffed blue elephant.

Trembling, she stooped down to lightly touch Ben, her fingers gentle against his brow. Her baby. Kahlil's baby. "I can't believe it's going to end like this."

Rifaat placed his hand on the top of the car door, stared down at her. "I am sorry, my lady."

Bryn couldn't speak.

"I know what he did, my lady, the sheikh's brother. I was there that night he attacked you in your room."

Her head jerked up, but still her voice failed her. Rifaat shook his own head once, slowly, wearily. "The surveillance cameras picked up that he'd entered the women's quarters. I didn't know what to do but then I heard you scream. I went into your room, and you were struggling, reaching for the jewelry box.''

Suddenly aspects of that night fell into place for Bryn, pieces of a difficult puzzle coming together. She'd wondered how she'd managed, how she'd escaped. ''I didn't knock him out. You did.''

''It had to be done.''

''Then you dragged Amin away.''

''I saw you leave the palace. I didn't stop you.'' Rifaat tapped the car door and stepped away. ''I've thought many times I should have told his highness about that night, but you'd run away, and Amin remained close with Kahlil. How to tell a sheikh that his brother is a fraud?''

It dawned on her then that Kahlil would always be vulnerable. Everyone wanted a piece of him. Everyone expected something. She felt Kahlil's impossible burden, and her chest squeezed tight. ''You can't,'' she said softly. ''You don't.''

''I'll talk to him now if you want.''

''And what? Turn Kahlil against you, too? I don't think so. I love him too much to have him live without at least one true friend, and you are his friend, Rifaat.''

''If I don't go to him, you'll lose him.''

''I've already lost him.'' She tried to smile but failed. ''Tell Kahlil—'' She stopped, cast a last lingering glance at the shuttered palace. ''Never mind. I better go before Ben wakes.''

# CHAPTER TWELVE

ONLY two weeks ago she had sat in this very soft, leather seat in the luxurious jet cabin, cradling her sleeping son. Now here she was again, returning to Texas, but Dallas was no longer home. Home was with Kahlil. Home was the three of them together.

The plane vibrated, engines on, noise unnervingly loud. She could smell a whiff of the fuel, and the green and white lights of the runway twinkled in the distance. They'd leave the gate any second now. Tears burned the back of her eyes, her throat raw and swollen from too much emotion.

How could it all end like this? For one night, that one blissful night of their second honeymoon, there'd been such hope. Instead it had all come apart—and she didn't know how to ever explain the truth to Kahlil, how to make him understand that her love for him was greater than her shortcomings, greater than her insecurities, greater than anything else in the world. Real love wasn't just passion, but faith. And yet Kahlil had no faith in her. No trust, either.

The engines thrust forward. The plane pulled away from the gate. Lights flickered, overhead lamps turning down.

It hurt, wild, raw, unjustly, that she lost him not just

once, but twice. She wanted to weep with the loss but knew if she let a single tear fall, she'd lose all control.

"If you go," a deep male voice rasped from the back of the cabin, "you must take me."

*Kahlil?*

Slowly, afraid to discover his voice was a figment of her imagination, she turned in her seat.

Kahlil stood in the back of the cabin, faded jeans, T-shirt. Red-rimmed eyes, hair disheveled, his face washed but bruised. "Don't go. Not without me."

She couldn't speak, a lump the size of Kentucky prevented her from uttering a word. Hot, gritty tears burned her eyes and she simply shook her head, unable to believe he was here, on the plane, even after everything that had happened.

"I can't do it," he added roughly. "I can't do this without you."

Her lips parted, her mouth trembled. She forced sound through her throat. "Do what?"

"Rule Zwar, or lead my people." His voice broke and he shoved his hand through his hair. "I don't know if I can even live, feeling like this."

"No—"

And still he hung back, in the soft shadows of the cabin. "I'm no better than my father. He said he always acted for the good of his people, but I don't know if that's true. He said rules—order—must always come first, but I've tried to live like that and it's unbearable. My life is unbearable."

She struggled to rise, wanting to go to him but she

still held Ben and at the moment her legs weren't strong enough to fully support both of them. "It can't be unbearable, not when people love you as much as we do."

Kahlil jerked forward. "So why do I have to hurt you? Why have I put us through this hell?"

"I don't know, but there's a reason, I'm sure."

"No, there's never a reason for being deliberately cruel." He stopped a foot away, his golden eyes haunted, his expression bleak. "I can't hurt you anymore. I have to stop, and I have to stop now."

"You're here now, that's what counts." She fought to swallow, the tumult of emotions almost overwhelming. She didn't know whether to be happy or angry that Rifaat had broken his word and gone to Kahlil. "Rifaat told you, then? I asked him not to."

Kahlil frowned. "Rifaat told me what?" His expression revealed his confusion. "Has something happened? Something to Ben?"

"No, nothing like that." She hesitated, realizing Kahlil obviously had no idea what she was talking about. So Rifaat didn't go to him...which meant Kahlil had come here on his own. For a moment she didn't know what to think, feel, and then suddenly something powerful in her heart broke loose and Bryn felt an intense wave of joy.

"How is he?" Kahlil asked, indicating Ben, moving forward to take him from her arms.

"Good. He's been asleep most the time."

"Poor little man." Kahlil cradled Ben close against his chest, muscles in his arms cording as he hugged his son. "Does he know what I did? Does Ben know I was sending you away?"

"He woke up earlier when we boarded the plane, but I didn't tell him where we were going. I just said we were taking a ride."

Kahlil's jaw jutted as he swallowed hard. "I don't know what I was thinking—I don't know how I could send you away like that. I was there on the other side of the door, listening to you cry." His sober gaze met hers. "I felt your hand on the door—there was heat, and pain—and yet instead of opening the door, I ignored you. I pretended you didn't exist." His mouth twisted, his expression raw. "It makes me sick. How could I do that to you? How could I do that to my family?"

"Probably some coping mechanism left over from your childhood," she answered faintly.

"Doesn't make it right. I'm sorry. Forgive me."

"There's nothing to forgive."

"There's plenty. We al-Assads are notoriously hard on our women."

Tears, gritty tears, pricked her eyes. She reached up to touch his face, moving her fingers down from his beautiful cheek to his angular jaw. "I love you."

"I know. And I know nothing happened between you and my brother. You're not that kind of a woman. Your heart is too pure. Besides, I know my brother. He's spent his life manipulating me, playing me. I can only imagine the hell he put you through."

"It's over now. We have Ben back, and I have you."

Abruptly Kahlil looked away, his jaw tightening.

"Tonight, when you screamed my name, it was the same way my mother had cried out for me. I didn't know then why she was being taken away, I just knew something awful was happening. I never saw her again."

He drew a deep painful breath, features contorted. "I had the chance once, when I was a teenager, visiting the States. But I refused to see her." He made a rough sound in the back of his throat. "She died less than a year later. Cancer."

"You didn't know."

"Refusing to see her was one of the worst mistakes I ever made. But I came close tonight to making another one." His head jerked around, his eyes bored into hers, searching, needing to know. "Your home is in Tiva with me, and I want you here with me. *If* that's what you want."

"I want," she whispered, fighting tears.

"I can't keep losing you."

"I've never wanted to go."

"Life is very hard—"

"I know. I want to spend forever with you. I want us to be together, for Ben, for each other."

"Good. Because I don't want Ben pulled between us. I couldn't bear for him to know what I've known." He drew a ragged breath. "The suffering did not make me stronger. It made me cruel. Please still love me."

"Oh, Kahlil, I do. I swear I do."

"No more separate rooms, no more harem and women's quarters. I just want you with me."

"Like a real couple?"

He nodded grimly, determined. "A normal couple, so we can do our best to give Ben a normal family. It's what he deserves, what every child deserves, and it's what I want most."

Her heart ached, tinged by bittersweet joy. "I love you."

"I love you more—"

"You can't!"

"I can. I'm the Sheikh Kahlil Hasim al-Assad, ruler of Zwar, leader of my people. Whatever I say goes." And leaning forward, Ben still tucked safely against his chest, he kissed her, tenderly. Reverently. "You can't fight it, love. You're not going to win."

These were the sweetest words in the world. Smiling through a blur of tears, Bryn threw up her hands. "Fine. I surrender!"

Copyright © Harlequin Enterprises Limited 1997
All rights reserved

**Modern Romance**™
...seduction and
passion guaranteed

**Tender Romance**™
...love affairs that
last a lifetime

**Sensual Romance**™
...sassy, sexy and
seductive

**Sizzling Romance**™
...sultry days and
steamy nights

**Medical Romance**™
...medical drama on
the pulse

**Historical Romance**™
...rich, vivid and
passionate

*29 new titles every month.*

*With all kinds of Romance for
every kind of mood...*

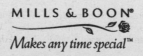

MILLS & BOON®

*Makes any time special*™

MAT3

# Coming Home

*Scandal drove David away*
*Now love will draw him home . . .*

# PENNY JORDAN

## Published 21st September

*Available at most branches of WH Smith, Tesco,*
*Martins, Borders, Easons, Sainsbury, Woolworth*
*and most good paperback bookshops*

MILLS & BOON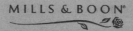

# Modern Romance™

**CLAIMING HIS MISTRESS** *by Emma Darcy*

When hot-shot financier Carver Dane attends a masked ball, he isn't expecting a fiery encounter with a woman who ignites the same desire he once knew with Katie Beaumont. The last time he felt such longing was ten years ago...

**A RICH MAN'S TOUCH** *by Anne Mather*

The arrival of wealthy businessman Gabriel Webb into Rachel's life is about to change everything! She isn't prepared when he touches emotions in her that she had carefully hidden away. But is Gabriel only interested in a fleeting affair?

**ROME'S REVENGE** *by Sara Craven*

Rome d'Angelo could have his pick of women, but his fiancée had already been chosen for him – by his grandfather. A family feud meant Rome must make Cory Grant his bride and then jilt her. But could he let her walk away?

**THE SICILIAN'S PASSION** *by Sharon Kendrick*

Kate was mistress to passionate Sicilian man, Giovanni Calverri. And that was all it was supposed to be – until the day fate forced them to put their steamy arrangement on hold and think about what they really had together...

## On sale 5th October 2001

*Available at most branches of WH Smith, Tesco, Martins, Borders, Easons, Sainsbury, Woolworth and most good paperback bookshops*

0901/01a

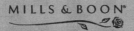

MILLS & BOON®

# Modern Romance™

**MARRIAGE ON THE AGENDA** by Lee Wilkinson

When Loris Bergman attended her father's party, she couldn't shake off the feeling that one of the men attending was familiar to her. Yet Jonathan Drummond insisted they were strangers! What exactly was on his agenda…?

**THE KYRIAKIS BABY** by Sara Wood

Emma will stop at nothing to claim her baby daughter back from Greek tycoon Leon Kyriakis — even if she has to share a bed with him once more…

**THE DEVIL'S BARGAIN** by Robyn Donald

Hope's stubborn independence had been threatened when she'd first met Kier Carmichael and sensed the powerful attraction between them. She had refused to succumb to his seduction, and set off to travel Australia. But five years later, Kier walks into her workplace, all suave sophistication and dark, stunning looks…

**DENIM AND DIAMONDS** by Moyra Tarling

Years ago sexy Kyle Masters had been severely tempted by Piper Diamond, but he'd sent her on her way — too honourable to snatch her innocence. Now Piper is back, and determined to make Kyle her husband — whatever it takes…

## On sale 5th October 2001

*Available at most branches of WH Smith, Tesco, Martins, Borders, Easons, Sainsbury, Woolworth and most good paperback bookshops*

0901/01b

# FREE
# 2 BOOKS
## AND A SURPRISE GIFT!

We would like to take this opportunity to thank you for reading this Mills & Boon® book by offering you the chance to take TWO more specially selected titles from the Sensual Romance™ series absolutely FREE! We're also making this offer to introduce you to the benefits of the Reader Service™—

★ FREE home delivery  ★ FREE gifts and competitions
★ FREE monthly Newsletter  ★ Exclusive Reader Service discounts
★ Books available before they're in the shops

Accepting these FREE books and gift places you under no obligation to buy; you may cancel at any time, even after receiving your free shipment. Simply complete your details below and return the entire page to the address below. ***You don't even need a stamp!***

**YES!** Please send me 2 free Sensual Romance™ books and a surprise gift. I understand that unless you hear from me, I will receive 4 superb new titles every month for just £2.49 each, postage and packing free. I am under no obligation to purchase any books and may cancel my subscription at any time. The free books and gift will be mine to keep in any case.

TIZEC

Ms/Mrs/Miss/Mr ................................................Initials ..........................................
BLOCK CAPITALS PLEASE

Surname ...................................................................................................................

Address ...................................................................................................................

.................................................................................................................................

.................................................................Postcode ...........................................

**Send this whole page to:**
**UK: FREEPOST CN81, Croydon, CR9 3WZ**
**EIRE: PO Box 4546, Kilcock, County Kildare (stamp required)**

Offer valid in UK and Eire only and not available to current Reader Service subscribers to this series. We reserve the right to refuse an application and applicants must be aged 18 years or over. Only one application per household. Terms and prices subject to change without notice. Offer expires 31st December 2001. As a result of this application, you may receive offers from other carefully selected companies. If you would prefer not to share in this opportunity please write to The Data Manager at the address above.

Mills & Boon® is a registered trademark owned by Harlequin Mills & Boon Limited.
Sensual Romance™ is a registered trademark used under licence.